# DYNAMITE DAZE

Outlaw Duke Santee finds it a golden opportunity when he meets a sacked railroad employee wanting to get even with the company. The gang boss offers to help him rob the Flagstaff Flyer. But Santee's inexperienced in using high explosives; the train's express car as well as its payroll shipment is destroyed. So the outlaw plans a rescue mission to liberate the dynamite man Lee Jago, little realising that this will ultimately bring him to justice.

ETHAN FLAGG

# DYNAMITE DAZE

*Complete and Unabridged*

LINFORD
*Leicester*

First published in Great Britain in 2010 by
Robert Hale Limited
London

First Linford Edition
published 2011
by arrangement with
Robert Hale Limited
London

British Library CIP Data

Flagg, Ethan.
   Dynamite daze. - - (Linford western library)
   1. Western stories.
   2. Large type books.
   I. Title II. Series
   823.9′2–dc22

ISBN 978–1–44480–510–9

Published by
F. A. Thorpe (Publishing)
Anstey, Leicestershire
Set by Words & Graphics Ltd.
Anstey, Leicestershire
Printed and bound in Great Britain by
T. J. International Ltd., Padstow, Cornwall
This book is printed on acid-free paper

# 1

## Accident?

Lee Jago was a respected construction engineer with the Standard Pacific Railroad. A tall, imposing figure, he commanded the respect of his men by not being afraid to get his hands dirty. One of only a handful of Oriental Americans to have attained such an eminent position, Lee enjoyed the privilege of rank and status it brought.

But events were conspiring that were to test severely his loyalty to the company when the Chinese side of his heritage took an unforeseen jolt.

The railroad wanted to push a branch line south to service the needs of the gold-mining community around Wickenburg. After much deliberation the proposal was mooted that a tunnel ten miles in length be cut through the

1

Weaver mountain range. The alternative would have meant a detour of sixty miles, the extended delay being unacceptable to the company hierarchy.

Only after the work had progressed for three miles was it discovered that the bedrock had changed from hard sandstone to a much more unstable amalgam of shale and slate. This meant that the use of high explosives was highly dangerous. As a result, extra Chinese labourers had to be taken on to complete the job manually. It was time-consuming. And in addition, expensive steel supports had to be installed to secure the weak roof.

The site manager in charge of the tunnel construction was plagued by worry. Bradley Straker was studying a plan fixed to the wall of his office which indicated how the work was progressing. It showed a significant slowdown since the work had gone manual.

Anxiety was written all over the angular, careworn face.

His left eye twitched. The waxed

moustache was in a constant state of animation. Straker felt as though he had aged ten years over the last few weeks. At this rate his bonus of $2,000 for early completion of the project was in serious jeopardy.

The company directors were pressing him to step up the pace. Barely concealed was the threat of demotion to the rail gangs should he fail.

Straker knew there was only one way to save his job and the lucrative bonus. It would mean cutting corners. But he had done that numerous times in the past to achieve deadlines. Why not on this occasion? What held him back were the possible implications of resorting to high explosives in such volatile circumstances.

But there was no other option.

Having made up his mind Straker went over to the door of the converted railway carriage. The man he was seeking had just come back from supervising the Chinese coolies clearing debris from the tunnel. One of them was receiving a severe tongue-lashing from the heavyweight foreman, who terminated the hectoring onslaught with a brutal clubbing.

'Don't talk back to me!' hollered the irate foreman raising his club for a further beating. 'I don't wanna hear no excuses. It's your job as charge hand to get them damn yeller bastards to clear all the rockfalls before they knock off for the day. If'n it happens tomorrow, I'll dock yer pay. Hear me?'

Straker smiled. He fully approved of Rafe Boondock's tactics, believing that physical threats and intimidation were the only means of driving the Chinese labourers to maintain their Herculean efforts. But he had more important issues in mind for which the foreman was admirably suited.

'Rafe!' he shouted attracting the stalwart bully's attention. 'Over here. We got things to discuss.'

The Chinese hand took the opportunity to scuttle away.

'Somethin' wrong, boss?' enquired

4

the bluff foreman somewhat anxiously. The cigar offered by his superior erased the notion that trouble was brewing.

Entering the converted Pullman carriage, Straker complemented the cigar with a glass of French brandy. Boondock had carried out clandestine affairs for the site manager on previous occasions. So there was no reason why he should not be amenable to the current proposal that Straker had in mind. Still, there was nothing like a good smoke and the finest liquor to help oil the wheels of progress, persuade a man towards your way of thinking.

Through the tendrils of blue smoke Straker appraised his confederate.

Boondock was a rough and ready Irishman, boasting an unruly mop of red hair beneath the black derby worn at a rakish angle. Bulging muscles gained from the heavy work involved in building railroads were barely con-cealed by the brown serge suit. Slouching back in an armchair opposite the manager, he was in no hurry to leave the opulent surroundings.

'I have another job for you, Rafe,' began the manager, playing the 'good buddies' card. 'It'll be worth a hefty bonus in your pay packet.' He paused, a loose smile creasing the oily visage as he noted Boondock's raised eyebrows. 'We need to speed up work on the tunnel.'

'I'm pushin' them blasted Chinks as much as I can.' The foreman waved his cigar around, indicating there was only so much labour he could get out of them. 'Without dynamite it's a slow job.'

It was Straker's turn now to raise an expressive eyebrow. Boondock latched on to his meaning straight away, although his ruddy kisser registered stark disbelief.

'You can't be meanin' — '

'Why not?' snapped the manager, eyes bright and challenging.

'Playin' with high explosives is no game of skittles. We're talkin' about a high-risk business here, Mr Straker,' argued the foreman. 'The roof might cave in.'

'But you agree that with a judicious use of dynamite, we could link up with the northbound phase, which Jago's crew are digging, by the end of the month?'

Boondock removed his hat. His scarred puss knitted like a patchwork quilt as he scratched his head in thought. The sinister undertones of the boss's suggestion needed some accepting. This was serious business, far more so than any previous skulduggery he had carried out.

A crafty gleam appeared in his emerald-green eyes. After due consideration of the issue he gave an acquiescent nod before adding quietly, almost as an afterthought, 'And what sort of bonus is it you be offerin', then?'

'I reckon a job like this is worth two hundred,' proposed Straker, smirking as he slung back the rest of the brandy.

Boondock emitted a grating guffaw.

'Don't make me laugh, mister!' There was no hint of the foreman's previous kowtowing in the brittle retort. 'I want five hundred and not a cent less,' he shot back, holding the manager with a gaze that defied him to refuse.

Straker's face assumed a rich purple hue. Flecks of spittle oozed from between his clenched teeth. Fists balled in fury. Tight-lipped, he seethed in silence knowing that the Irishman had him over a barrel. If the job was to be completed on time, he needed the foreman's active co-operation.

'OK,' he whispered in a barely concealed growl. 'You got yourself a deal. Just make certain that tunnel gets dug.'

'You can count on me . . . *sir*.' Boondock grinned. 'Let's shake on it.'

Straker grudgingly accepted the proffered hand which engulfed his own tiny paw in a vicelike grip. Slow and deliberate pressure was then applied. Straker's face remained blank, devoid of expression. The last thing he wanted was to accord the tough Irishman any satisfaction.

With a deft flourish and a lurid smile, Boondock eventually let go. He tipped his hat, then snatched up a handful of cigars from the solid silver humidor on the desk and swaggered out into the warmth of early evening. There was a brisk lightness in his step as he sauntered across to the foremen's canteen.

Back in the carriage Straker mopped the sweat from his brow as he massaged his bruised appendage. He hated being outmanoeuvred. When this business had been concluded he would need to reappraise the position of Rafe Boondock.

'Nobody makes a fool of Bradley D. Straker,' snarled the manager into his refilled glass of brandy. 'And certainly no damned Irish bogtrotter.'

He hawked a plug of phlegm into the spitoon over in the corner. An unfortunate accident could easily be arranged. The welcome notion cleared the turbulence from Brad Straker's disturbed brain. Helped by a few more snorts of brandy, he felt positively buoyed up, once again in full control.

* * *

Engineer Lee Jago cocked his head. Frown lines ribbed his sweat-stained brow. He had felt a slight tremor under his feet. Lee was supervising the controlled explosions that were necessary to ensure the right amount of sandstone was dislodged from the parent bedrock. It needed to be spot on to ensure the work progressed on an even camber.

So far the tunnel at his end had been pushed two miles through the Weaver range. His crew were making good progress to link up with the southbound sector. But Lee was well aware that very soon the volatile nature of the rock system would change, forcing the work-rate down to that of a plodding donkey.

There it was again.

If he didn't know better, Lee would

have sworn that the tremor was caused by an explosion. Only faint, the noise was clearly some distance off. Although it appeared to be taking place in the direction of the other tunnel link. He shrugged the ludicrous idea off. Dynamite had been abandoned once the other team had encountered the shifting gravel and shale.

Maybe the noise was from a mine working. There were certainly a number of outfits digging for gold in these mountains. Then again, it could be the bedrock shifting. His own use of explosives meant that audible detection of the strange phenomenon was intermittent.

Straker was well aware that Lee Jago would kick up a stink if he realized the devious game that was being played out. And the nearer the two tunnels came to joining up, the more chance there was of that half-breed engineer arriving at the obvious conclusion.

He could not allow that to happen.

The answer was to pull him off the

11

job. He therefore dispatched a message instructing Jago to head south and begin surveying the country through which the line would pass *en route* to Wickenburg.

Jago was somewhat puzzled as to the reasoning behind this abrupt change of plan. But, nonetheless, he complied.

★   ★   ★

Two weeks later the tunnels achieved a near perfect link-up. It was a moment for celebration.

'We done it, boss!' Rafe Boondock said with a grin as he accepted a glass of champagne. 'And two days ahead of schedule as well.'

The two scheming rogues toasted their success.

Straker was already thinking of the directorship that the managing director had promised should he deliver on time.

'This is only the beginning, Rafe,' asserted the construction manager.

'Once I'm firmly ensconced on the board, there'll be plenty of opportunity to earn more valuable commissions from contract tenders.'

'You won't be forgettin' old Rafe, now, will you, Mr Straker,' hissed the foreman charily, 'when the bonuses are handed out?'

Straker clapped his associate on the shoulder.

'You're my second-in-command now, Rafe,' he guffawed loudly, an evil glint in his beady eye. 'Stick with me and the only way to go is up.' He omitted to add that in Boondock's case the 'up' in question would be the proverbial creek, and without a paddle, courtesy of a large helping of dynamite.

A commotion outside the carriage halted the toasting.

'What in tarnation is that ruckus?' demanded Straker. An urgent knocking on the office door brought a petulant frown to his flaccid features. 'Come in!' he rasped.

A small man entered, tugging off his

hat. Harsh breath rasped in the jigger's dry throat as he attempted to impart some dire news. He had clearly been running.

'What is it, man?' snapped Straker impatiently. 'What the hell's happened?'

'Its the tunnel,' gasped the messenger, sucking air into rasping lungs. 'There's been a rockfall at the six-mile point.'

'How bad is it?' jumped in Boondock, grabbing the man by the collar and roughly shaking him. 'Out with it, yer little turd.'

'Bad enough,' panted a nervous Harpo Chanter. 'The roof collapsed while the Chinks were clearing up the debris ready for laying the track.'

The foreman's eyes swivelled towards his partner in collusion.

'Any killed?' asked the manager, his face a blank mask.

'The charge engineer reckons about twenty.'

Straker ground his teeth, then gave a non-commital shrug. He considered for a moment before replying.

But he was not contemplating the grief such a disaster would bring to the families of those involved. Securing the promised bonus for finishing the job on time was of more importance. The fact that twenty human beings had been crushed to death on account of his double-dealing he regarded with cold indifference. After all, they were only Chinks with no rights under American law, and could easily be replaced.

'We can soon get extra labour sent down from the Flagstaff depot,' he said, dragging hard on a dead cigar. 'It'll only set us back a couple of days.'

Straker tossed a five-dollar gold piece to the hovering messenger.

'Have a drink on me, Harpo.' He smiled. 'You done well getting over here so quick.'

'Gee, thanks, boss,' gasped the weasel, backing out of the door. His mind was already focusing on a full bottle of genuine Scotch whisky.

When the little guy had departed

Straker issued new orders to his confederate. 'Get that rockfall cleared. Then have someone collect the bodies.'

He took out a billfold, and extracted a twenty-dollar note and handed it to Boondock. 'This should pay for some wreaths and the burials. Pine coffins only, and no extras.' Then, spearing his associate with a baleful glare, he added, 'And make sure everybody knows it's the company that's paying. And we deeply regret such a terrible accident.'

The foreman nodded. 'I understand, boss. You can rely on me.'

'And get a repair detail on to shoring up that collapsed roof section. I wanna be laying track through the tunnel in three days.'

Boondock reached for the brandy decanter. He was about to pour himself a glass when Straker rapped out curtly, 'What you waiting for, then? Christmas?'

'Oh! Y-yeh! S-sorry, boss,' stuttered the reproved foreman as Straker brusquely ushered him out of the office. 'I'll get on to it straight away.'

# 2

## The Noble Gesture

It was two days later before Lee Jago heard about the so-called accident. He was surveying the terrain over which the next section of track would be laid when the supply locomotive driver leaned out of his cab and called down to him.

'Did you hear about the tunnel accident?' A puzzled look encouraged the driver to continue: 'Seems like the roof collapsed, killing a number of coolies.'

Jago stiffened. 'Any reason given?' he asked, although the answer was already hammering at his brain cells.

'It was in that weakened sector,' replied the driver in a matter-of-fact tone. He had no idea that Jago was of Chinese descent. Lee's physical appearance had favoured his American mother's side of the family. 'I heard tell they'd started usin' dynamite agin.' The guy shook his head sadly. 'Poor sods never stood a chance.'

Lee's broad shoulders slumped.

'Did . . . did any get out?' The words emerged as a choking retch.

'Far as I know, they were all killed.'

Lee turned away to hide the overwhelming despair that threatened to engulf him. His brother-in-law and a cousin had been members of that crew. How was he going to break the news to his wife? Chuan Li would be devastated.

Tears etched a trail down his weathered face. For a full five minutes he was unable to think beyond the stark grief of his loss and that of his countrymen.

Then, slowly, reason began to push aside the grey mush of the brutally shocking revelation. Dark eyes the colour of burnt oak narrowed to thin slits as the surveyor squared his broad shoulders and drew himself up to his full height of six feet two.

So it had been dynamite that his acute hearing had picked up in the tunnel. Then the next piece of the puzzle fell into place. Bradley Straker had deliberately moved him out of the south link to avoid a confrontation and the unwelcome publicity such unscrupulous procedures would have courted.

The bastard had murdered his kin.

'When are you heading back to base?' Lee's query to the supply driver was waspish and delivered with more than a hint of venom.

The driver could see that the surveyor had been deeply affected by the grave tidings, although he did not know the reason.

'Once the supplies have been unloaded, we can head off back without delay,' he said. 'Shouldn't be more'n two hours.'

'You'll have a extra passenger.'

★　★　★

Once the train had arrived back at base, Lee wasted no time. He jumped off before it had stopped and made a beeline for the railroad office.

A line of coolies passed by on the far side of the track, their backs bent under the weight of heavy picks and shovels. Small in stature, they were nonetheless the backbone of the railroad's incessant drive to open up the frontier. Lee felt a sense of pride in his countrymen and their heritage of hard work and industry.

Then it occurred to him that these must be the replacements for the dead men. His granite features hardened.

Without bothering to knock he barged straight into the office.

Three men were hunched over a set of plans. Straker was discussing the next section of the project with two other line managers.

Lounging on a sofa in the corner was a blunt-faced roughneck whom Lee recognized. His stony features seemed carved in a bitter scowl. No effort was made to conceal his dislike of the unscrupulous foreman. He had crossed swords with Rafe Boondock once before when the scheming toady had belaboured a coolie for slaking his thirst without asking permission.

Boondock returned the odious glower. His hand strayed to the scar above his right eye where Jago had returned the favour.

'What is the meaning of this interruption?' demanded Straker. 'This is a private meeting. If you want to see me, make an appointment with my secretary.' He dismissed the intruder with a wave of the hand, then returned to the matter under deliberation.

But Jago refused to be pushed aside so easily. He stood his ground.

'Was there something else?' sneered the manager, affecting his most disdainful manner.

'Why was I not consulted about the use of dynamite in the north tunnel?' he said, trying to maintain an even timbre to his voice. 'Those men were my responsibility. As charge engineer I should have been informed of any changes to the digging procedure.'

'As I recall,' snorted Straker, squaring his shoulders and adjusting his necktie, 'you were put in charge of the forward survey team. The excavation of the tunnels was no longer your concern.'

Jago's face tightened. His checks assumed an angry tinge of red.

'You did that, knowing I would strongly object to the use of high explosives in such volatile conditions.' Lee could barely contain his anger.

Straker's shoulders lifted in a shrug of unconcern. A loose smile played across the unctuous features as he attempted to defuse the tense situation.

'Why are you making all this fuss?' scoffed the manager. 'Your job is to build this rail extension in the shortest possible time. And if that means having to sacrifice a few coolies . . . ' He left the sentence unfinished, then glanced at his colleagues for their support.

The other two managers nodded their agreement.

'Rest assured, Jago,' purred a short, balding dude with tufts of black hair sprouting between prominent ears, 'these fellows have been given a coffin burial. And at the company's expense, I might add.'

'Not to mention flowers,' added the other one.

This seemed to satisfy any conscience they might have acknowledged.

Lee was too stunned to reply.

Boondock levered himself out of the chair.

'Just go back to what yer paid for, Jago,' he hissed, slapping a wooden club in to the palm of his hand. There was no mistaking the hardcase's meaning, and his obvious intention should the intruder continue his unwelcome remonstration. 'Getting the job done is what matters here. Not saving the hides of some miserable Chinks.'

Blood rushed to Lee's head. A red mist of vengeance threatened to swamp any attempt at lucidity. He couldn't believe what he was hearing. The

United States of America was meant to be a land of equality for all men. Clearly some were regarded more equal than others.

On the outside Lee's dusky profile remained a stony mask, deadpan and unreadable. But inside he was a seething confusion of turbulent emotions. All his instincts screamed out to gain justice for his deceased countrymen. There was nothing more he would have liked than to wipe the smarmy grin off Straker's sneering visage.

Every muscle in his body was drawn tight as a bowstring. He was within a whisker of letting fly.

Luckily, commonsense prevailed.

This was not the time to lose his temper. Lee knew that he would be the loser in any fracas. Rafe Boondock would be more than pleased to ensure it would be his blood that was spilled.

'I'm sorry that you take this attitude, gentlemen,' he murmured, barely above a whisper, while trying to ignore the shabby foreman.

His bunched fists slowly uncoiled as he swung on his heel and quickly made a dignified exit.

'And next time, make an appointment.' The caustic guffaw from the foreman was accompanied by a bout of muted laughter as the door slammed shut.

Lee staggered down the steps of the car and made his way over to the supervisors' mess. He was shaking and badly needed a drink to calm his shattered nerves.

One thing was for certain. No way were these dog-turds going to escape their just desserts.

All that needed sorting out now was the how and the when. And the sooner the better. But it would need to look like a tragic accident.

$\star$   $\star$   $\star$

A hint of light filtered through the window blind of the shack that Lee shared with three other engineers. Sleep had been fitful. He had tossed and turned throughout the night, his head filled with all manner of schemes to achieve his end. Most were chimeric pipedreams. Others were unfeasible without the blame falling squarely on to his shoulders.

For his wife's sake, he had to make it look like an accident.

There had to be an answer.

It was only when he was heading for the chow tent next morning that the perfect solution struck home. As he ambled along the main east-west railway track, he noticed that Straker's office car was located on a branch siding that ran parallel to the main through line. And at either end were a set of points.

His dark eyes burned with a fearsome brilliance.

After filling his plate he headed over to a corner table. He was in no mood for desultory conversation. The clatter of cutlery on tin plates went unheeded. Lee had no appetite. Idly playing with his food the essence of a plan formed in his foxy brain. Anxiously the engineer peered around the mess tent to ensure that nobody had been a witness to his sudden euphoric bearing.

For the plan to be a success the railroad camp had to be empty. That meant waiting for all the workers to leave. It also meant that he would have to go into hiding for the next hour.

Lee pulled out his watch and checked the time.

7.24 a.m.

The early Flyer was due past at 8.42 a.m.

More than enough time to do the business.

Affecting an air of casual indifference, Lee walked out of the tent and made his way over to the dynamite store. It was the ideal place of concealment, as any requisite explosives were always procured the night before. A quick glance around to ensure he was unobserved, then he stepped inside and relocked the door. Now all he had to do was wait. Always the hardest part.

For the next half-hour, Lee hid behind some boxes. With each approaching sound of voices, he held his breath, not daring to move a muscle. At last all was quiet. The work crews had all departed.

Time to get moving. The grating of a rusty hinge as he carefully opened the door seemed to hammer at his taut senses. Five cactus wrens flew past, alighting on the roof of the isolated managerial car. Watchers that were in for a startling surprise if they remained there. And so was Bradley D. Straker. It was well known that the contract manager never rose before nine o'clock in the morning.

Lee's face cracked wide in a darkly sardonic smile that lacked any hint of levity.

'You're gonna get one heck of a wake-up call, Mr Manager,' murmured the engineer to himself.

Narrowed eyes revealed to Jago that, of human witnesses, there was thankfully none.

Bending low, he hustled across to the

rail points lever where the up line branched off. Grasping a firm hold of the steel handle, he jerked it towards his body. With little more than a creaking rasp, the line change was effected. Still nobody in view.

The far end of the siding was 200 yards away. To avoid being spotted by Brad Straker or any of his associates, it was necessary to make a wide detour behind the disparate array of huts and storage yards that comprised the base camp.

8.25 a.m.

In his room at the end of the supervisors' block, Rafe Boondock yawned and stretched. His head felt like it had been kicked by an obdurate mule. He groaned aloud.

'Never again,' he moaned, head in hands. It was his usual vow to avoid rotgut whiskey in future.

Scratching the ample belly bulging from beneath a grubby one-piece undershirt, the hung-over foreman staggered to his feet. He should have been on the early shift today. A bottle of genuine Scotch had persuaded his mate Tom Bell to cover for him. Just so long as Straker didn't find out.

As he went lurching over to the dresser, his ears picked up an alien noise outside the hut. Something that oughtn't to be there. It sounded like the shuffling of boots on gravel. Boondock's ugly puss twisted in a quizzical frown.

Was there some other turkey taking an unofficial day off? Only one way to find out.

8.36 a.m.

Lee quickened his pace. The down-line points were just beyond the next hut. He anxiously noted that it was the one where the foremen slept. But they were all away on the job by now.

He scurried round the side, then broke into a run on reaching open ground with no more cover. His atuned ears picked up the rumble of the Flagstaff Flyer, no more than a few minutes away. He had timed it to perfection.

Boondock's eyes widened.

What in thunder was that blasted engineer doing here? And heading over to the points. What was his game?

Then it struck the foreman. Instantly, he threw off the lethargic torpor that seconds before was claiming his body. Grabbing a hold of his club, Boondock slammed out of the shack. But he was too late. Jago was already working the lever of the points. And the Flyer was rattling down the straight. In less than a minute it would divert on to the siding.

Maybe if he clubbed the unsuspecting engineer he could reverse the points. Then it occurred to him that the up section would also have been changed.

Straker didn't stand a chance.

'Mr Straker!' he yelled, waving his arms impotently. 'Wake up! Get out of there!'

But his words were drowned out by the thunderous rumble of the speeding locomotive as it veered on to the branch line. The ground shook as the two men were enveloped in steam. In seconds it had slammed into the managerial car, which disintegrated in a violent upheaval. Slivers of matchwood flew every which way like confetti at a giant's wedding.

The collision barely registered as the train continued on its way, rejoining the main track lower down. The squeal of the brake being applied by the driver indicated that it had not gone unnoticed in the cab. Sparks flew as the great iron monster slid down the rails, finally shuddering to a halt a half-mile down the track.

So intent was Lee on ensuring that his plan succeeded that he had failed to perceive the approach of his nemesis.

Boondock's mouth gaped wide as he saw his life on easy street, and the perks it had brought, disappearing along with the wrecked carriage. Nothing was left to indicate that, moments before, a large Pullman had stood there. Even the Bogey wheels had disappeared.

And it was all down to that conscience-stricken Chink engineer.

A murderous intent was etched

across the foreman's rough features.

Hefting the large club he charged at the unsuspecting perpetrator.

'Aaaaaagh!'

The throaty roar alerted Lee to the danger bearing down from his rear. He swung to face the attack.

But too late.

A mighty swipe from the heavy bludgeon connected with his exposed head knocking him senseless. Lee tumbled to the ground.

Boondock stood over the stricken form, breathing heavily. The brutal club, already dripping with the blood of its victim, rose into the early morning air ready to deliver the *coup de grâce*.

A sixth sense stayed the vicious foreman's hand. Taking the varmint alive could be to his advantage. Gain him some credence with the company. He could always claim he had come back to camp for extra supplies when questioned. And seeing the bastard hanging from a rope would be icing on the cake. He would enjoy nothing better than watching the jury deliver a guilty verdict.

A lurid smirk split the pockmarked kisser as he grabbed a hold of Lee's long back hair and unceremoniously dragged him back to the shack.

# 3

## Chance Encounter

It was an hour after sun-up.

Duke Santee didn't need to look at his watch. A loose smile creased the gang leader's swarthy features. He had judged their arrival at Fresnal Gap in Northern Arizona to perfection. The train robbers were splayed out side by side along the upper rim of the deep ravine, awaiting the arrival of the Flagstaff Flyer.

Had he paused to consider the notion, Santee might have reserved judgement on labelling the gang 'train robbers'. This was in fact their very first foray into that extremely lucrative, though no less dangerous, arena of banditry. But Duke Santee was confident of being able to relieve the train of its valuable cargo.

Having agreed the plan of action, the

gang were more than eager to partici-
pate in this new venture.

Democratic discussion had always
been a fervent Santee trait provided, of
course, that nobody objected to his
submissions. And train robbery was
most definitely a step up the dubious
ladder of lawless endeavour. A feather
in their hats. Added to which the boss
had given a firm assurance that the
contents of the express car would be
sufficient to set them all up for a life of
leisure.

The idea had been formulated during
a chance meeting with a disgruntled
railroad employee who had recently
been sacked for late time-keeping. This
innocuous, rather sickly-looking weasel
just happened to be drowning his sor-
rows in the company of a bottle of hooch
in Ash Fork when Santee shouldered
his way into the Galloping Goose saloon.

Greenbacks from a successful, if somewhat meagrely rewarded stagecoach hold-up
near Tucson were burning a hole in his
pocket.

In accordance with their usual practice, the gang had split up after the robbery, agreeing to meet back at their hideout on the banks of Buffalo Wash when the loot ran out. But 200 bucks apiece was not likely to stretch very far. In consideration of this, Santee had ordered them to be back at the cabin by the end of the month.

Smoke hung in the fusty air of the dimly lit saloon. The smell of stale cigar smoke and rotgut whiskey blended with that of unwashed bodies. Nobody appeared to notice the odious reek. After all, this was a drinking den, not some fancy-pants boudoir.

Duke Santee elbowed through to the bar, where he ordered a large beer. The babble of conversation went unheeded.

The gang leader was in pensive mood. It was always the case when a job had gone off smoothly. Maybe it had not yielded the payout he would have expected, but Santee always ensured that he acquired the lion's share — half for him, the rest divided equally amongst his cohorts. If they didn't like it, too bad. There was always the open door, or a chunk of hot lead for those who threatened his authority.

That had happened two months before. A half-breed, going under the name of Shalako, had challenged Santee's leadership qualities. Two well-placed bullets in the back of the head had cut short the critter's snarling defiance. And it had effectively silenced any further remonstrance from others who might have harboured similar inclinations.

Regular gang members held their peace. They were well aware that Duke Santee had the knack of sniffing out easy targets. They might not pay too well, but the pay was regular. And thus far, nobody had been caught in the line of fire.

Santee had kept the gang one step ahead of the law for over two years. It was a solid record.

In the year of 1880 the Western frontier was becoming increasingly hostile to the lawless breed of roughnecks that had once ruled the roost. Pinkertons and Arizona Rangers were becoming much more organized. Most towns now had their own law-enforcement agencies.

And then there was the telegraph. A monumental curse to all outlaw bands. Messages could be dispatched at the push of a key to warn of impending shipments or fleeing brigands.

Santee was well aware that murmurings in the gang were questioning the recent lack of big rewards. Laramie Wixx, a young hothead from Wyoming, had voiced their grumbles only the day before.

'Let me buy you a drink, partner.'

The slurred offer penetrated Santee's ruminations. It had originated from a stunted guy to his right. Santee couldn't help noting the little fellow's hangdog expression. Something was clearly bugging him.

'Some'n got under your craw, mister?' he enquired, casually accepting the glass of bourbon which he tossed down in a single gulp. A warm glow settled itself across his innards.

'Darned right there is,' snapped the testy dude, splashing another shot into Santee's empty glass. 'The blasted rail company, that's what!'

'Yeah?' replied Santee, although he was only half listening.

'Ain't they just gone and given me the push?' No answer was needed. 'And just cos I was a few minutes late. I tell yuh, buddy, it ain't fair.' He took a long swig from the neck of the half-empty bottle before resuming his choleric diatribe. A leering snarl twisted the little guy's ratlike features. He wagged a finger at his new pal. 'But nobody sacks Hyram T. Falmer without gettin' their fingers burned.'

'What yuh gonna do about it?' asked Santee, gently extracting the liquor bottle from the rodent's hand and helping himself. Free booze was not to be refused.

Falmer replied with a wry smirk, tapping his protuberant snout suggestively.

His companion shrugged.

'So what was your job?' he said, not caring one way or the other. Just keep the greenhorn plying him with liquor.

'Most important job with the company,' huffed Falmer, pompously squaring his narrow shoulders.

Santee raised his eyes to the yellowed ceiling. He was rapidly getting bored with this smarmy runt.

'Out with it then, Hyram,' he sighed.

A wide grin split the thin face.

'Consignment clerk.'

Suddenly Duke Santee was all ears.

*Consignment clerk.*

He was the guy who processed all the information regarding shipments, from barrels of nails, through slabs of salted beef, bolts of cloth to . . . *payroll shipments!*

'I know every damned thing that's headin' down the line for the next month,' burbled the soused clerk. 'East or west, Hyram knows best.' The guy's face creased up with laughter at his own wit.

Santee joined in.

Struggling to contain his excitement, the gang leader nonchalantly posed the vital question.

'Anything of . . . erm . . . particular importance being moved in the near future?' he asked, coughing to hide the edginess in his voice.

'Sure is,' came back the ex-clerk with verve. 'The biggest durned cash shipment this year. The miners at Wickenhurg ain't been paid for six months. So that's one mighty big payroll on the move.'

Santee's piercing brown eyes narrowed. The gang had never previously considered robbing a train. It had seemed out of their league. But with the inside information available to Falmer, the stakes had been raised substantially. Examining the slack-jawed profile of his companion, Santee considered how best to handle this heaven-sent opportunity.

The granite features tightened. Gently he guided the weasel away from the bar towards a secluded booth in the far corner of the room.

After peering round to ensure no twitching ears were listening in, the wily gang leader tentatively made his play.

'I take it you want to get even with the company for what they done,' he suggested in a low voice injected with enough intrigue to grab the guy's attention.

'Damn right I do.' The little guy disgustedly hawked a gob of phlegm into the matted straw covering the floor.

'Then maybe I can help you out.'

Falmer lifted a wispy eyebrow, the angular face creased with wary caution. Nonetheless, he was more than interested if retribution against his former employer was being proposed. A cunning glint replaced the previous glassy expression, the alcoholic fuzz being quickly discarded.

Once he had hooked the trout, Santee outlined his proposal.

An hour later an agreement had been reached that Hyram T. Falmer would receive a quarter share of the take. It was then merely a question of working out a plan of action.

'Leave that to me, Hyram.' A well-satisfied Duke Santee grinned. 'Me and the boys know just the place to pull this heist off.'

If the caper succeeded, it could be the making of them all. A dreamy expression suffused the outlaw's weathered contours. Visions of an opulent lifestyle on easy street fuelled his lurid imagination. He saw an endless stream of high-class dames tending to his every need in the finest hotel in San Francisco; flunkeys dancing to his tune; the best tailor-made duds.

He stood up, swayed slightly — more from the euphoric aura than the imbibed liquor. Fixing his black Stetson at a jaunty angle, he addressed his new partner. 'We'll meet up at the cabin one week from now,' he said. 'You know how to reach Buffalo Wash?'

Falmer nodded, awarding himself a hearty slug to celebrate his good fortune.

Before leaving, Santee grabbed his

new associate by the arm, his grip solid and uncompromising. His implacable gaze held the little man in a mesmeric grip.

'And not a word about this to anyone. You hear me, fella?' he hissed. The biting tone, barely above a whisper, was no less menacing for that. The consequences, should the scheme become public knowledge, were patently evident. Santee's Army Remington pistol jabbing at Falmer's hairy nose saw to that.

Colour drained from the runt's face. Pale-grey eyes bulged fearfully.

'S-sure thing, Duke,' he stammered. 'My lips are sealed.'

Santee relaxed. He holstered his lethal weapon with a flourish and smoothed down the little guy's ruffled coat.

'Just so's we both know the score.' He smirked before bidding the little guy a cheery farewell. Snatching up the bourbon he imbibed a hefty slug then sauntered out into the afternoon sun, bottle in hand.

# 4

## Fresnal Gap

Even at this early hour the sun was already burning into the backs of the three men straddling the edge of Pocatello Mesa. A bank of white mist clung to the floor of Fresnal Gap where the heat had not yet penetrated. It effectively blocked any sighting of the rail track that cut through the mile-long gash in the mountain fastness of the Mogollons.

Duke Santee was not worried. He knew it would lift within the next thirty minutes. More than enough time to eyeball the approach of the westbound Flyer.

He loosened the long army coat. Patched and repaired in numerous places, it was the gang leader's pride and joy. He never went on a job without

46

this emblem of distinction. It had become his calling-card. A fading gold collar star proclaimed the august wearer to have been a major in the army of the Confederate States of America.

Even though the War had been over for fifteen years, Santee still insisted on proudly wearing the uniform of his choice. It had led to him being nicknamed the 'Major', a title he was more than happy to acknowledge.

What he had failed to divulge to anyone was that Duke Santee had not risen beyond the rank of a lowly corporal in charge of trench digging with the 21st Tennessee Foot.

The major's uniform had been surreptitiously acquired following the end of hostilities when he had chanced upon a group of forgotten cadavers secreted in a pine thicket. They had clearly been missed by the corpsemen delegated to seek out and bury such casualties that now littered the abandoned war zone.

The decision to adopt this new

persona, together with a fictional and luridly heroic background to accompany it, was taken without any compunction. 'Major' Santee's conscience troubled him not a jot.

The bullet holes were no problem. Indeed, they added a smack of authenticity to the whole charade. And with a smart grey officer's hat and the latest six shooter to complete the outfit Duke Santee was ready to make the newly constituted United States pay a high price for its victory.

'Any chance of a brew before the action begins, Major?'

The halting enquiry came from his left.

Chip Flannery screwed his eyes into a thin line against the glare as he peered speculatively at the boss.

Chip was short for Chippendale; his parents were wealthy landowners from Kentucky. His mother's favourite piece of furniture was the ornately carved writing-desk made by the celebrated English furniture-maker. Chip had been destined for the high life. That plan was abruptly cut short when his doting father passed away.

The man who quickly assumed the head of the table at Flannery Towers lost no time in changing things to suit his personal whims. Shrugging off his new wife's entreaty that Chippendale should receive an education worthy of his standing in the community, the bullish overlord forced the boy into working the family coalmine.

But he had not reckoned with Chip's headstrong nature. The lad's self-control finally snapped when his stepfather raised a hand to him once too often. A chamberful of hot lead from his own Peacemaker was the brute's reward. From that day the young Chip was forced into a life on the run.

Santee's gaze remained focused on the distant horizon, from where the train would appear. A thin smile softened the hard profile. *Major*. Even after all these years, being thus addressed always engendered a heady feeling of elation.

'What d'yuh say, boss?' pressed another desperado to his right, a stocky Texas redneck appropriately labelled T-Bone Crocker. 'We got plenty of time before the Flyer's due. A smoke wouldn't go amiss, neither.'

A languid eye fastened on to the rotund outlaw.

'Make it quick!' Santee growled. Then, with a sharp-edged snap. 'But no quirlies! I ain't about to give that loco driver any advanced warnin'. Them fellas have eyes keener than a hungry buzzard.' Crocker grimaced but knew better than to argue. 'And send Falmer up here,' added Santee. 'I got some details to check over with him.'

In company with the well-rounded T-Bone Crocker, Flannery slid crabwise down the back slope to where their newest recruit was minding the horses.

'And make sure the critter brings me a mug of coffee.' The curt order chased him down to where the mounts were tethered.

Falmer had balked at having to

accompany the gang on their latest foray. But Santee had laid it on the line that his share of the proceeds was dependent on full, hands-on co-operation. The smarmy ex-clerk had huffed some but had been given little choice in the matter.

Of the remaining two gang members, Laramie Wixx had been sent back up the line to position himself on a vantage point known as the Devil's Elbow. It afforded the best place for observing the approach of the Flyer. Once it had been spotted, Wixx's instructions were to spur back and impart the good tidings. Santee estimated that his arrival would allow them twenty minutes to make the final preparations for the heist.

Shotgun Charlie Padora was secreted beyond Fresnal Gap where the train would finally come to a halt. The double-gauge Greener that never left his person would be an effective deterrent for anyone who might decide to investigate the loss of the express car. Cut down to half its manufactured length for maximum spread of shot, the twin-barrelled firearm was housed in a purpose-made scabbard strapped to Padora's back.

Poor sight occasioned by a stray piece of shell fragment during the Battle of Gettysburg had meant a regular six-shooter was no use to the old veteran. The lethal Greener effectively made up for any shortcomings.

Now all they had to do was wait. Always the hardest part of any caper.

Guns were rechecked. The sticks of dynamite and fuses for blowing open the heavy iron safe containing the booty were all present. According to Falmer, the timings were correct.

High explosives had never previously been used by the Santee Gang. The sole indication of Duke's nervous regard for such a heavyweight approach was a thin film of sweat coating his upper lip. Fortunately it was concealed by the thick, bushy moustache.

'You certain that we'll need this stuff to get the loot?' he asked, not for the first time, while sipping the thick Arbuckle brew.

Falmer concealed a sigh of irritation. 'Ain't I told yuh?' he grouched. 'The brakeman never carries a key. And for just such a reason as this. Only someone from Company head office and the mine manager can open the safe. And it will be screwed down to the floor. No way can one of them heavy dudes be moved.' He shrugged, shaking his head to emphasize that there was no other means of achieving their objective. 'The only way to get at the payroll is to blow the darned thing wide open.'

That was when a dust-caked apparition scuttled up the back slope and dropped down beside them. Noting the arrival of Wixx, the other two outlaws hustled up the slope. Heads ducked low, five sets of gritty orbs strained to be first to catch sight of the approaching train.

'It's on time,' announced Laramie Wixx, a wide grin splitting his wizened features. 'And there are only two freight cars ahead of the express van. This is gonna be like taking candy from a baby.'

The recent arrival didn't wait for a reply.

'*Hasta la vista*,' he hollered, quickly disappearing down the back slope. His place now was at the far end of Fresnal Gap to support Shotgun Charlie with any gunplay that might be needed.

Another five minutes passed before the plaintive shriek of the locomotive whistle announced the imminent arrival of the Flagstaff Flyer.

A plume of black smoke was the first indication that the train was approaching. Minutes later, the regular splutter and clank of the iron horse invaded the stillness of early morning. As it neared the deep ravine the driver once again heralded their advent with a mournful tug on the whistle.

'That has to he Huojin Soo a-drivin' that beauty,' proclaimed Hyram Falmer. 'The only Chinese loco driver in the company's employ.'

Santee lifted his eyebrows in surprise. 'How in a month of Sundays can you know somep'n like that,' he asked.

The weasel gave a superior sniff.

'By the tone of the whistle. Old Soo inserted an extra reed to give it that distinctive lonesome wail.'

All locomotive men took pride in the appearance of their charge and that included the individuality of the whistle tone. This guy was no exception. Driving wheels and a cow-catcher painted bright red blended perfectly with the green boiler and black balloon smokestack, now unremittingly belching forth. A golden plate at the front proclaimed the train to be Arizona's most prestigious — the celebrated Flagstaff Flyer.

This particular one, however, was a special: an extra delivery slotted into the schedule specifically for the purpose of conveying the vital payroll to Flagstaff. Normal trains had more coaches for passengers, including first-class Pullmans.

Santee was more concerned with the type of express car at the rear, in which the safe was located. He gave a visible sigh of relief after observing that it lacked the usual cupola. The raised lookout post, had there been one, would have enabled the brakeman to spot any sign of trouble ahead.

Santee smiled to himself. Little did the guy suspect what was about to befall him.

Wheezing and chugging like an angry buffalo, the veteran workhorse rattled into the steep-sided cutting, its harsh and discordant clamour jarring the eardrums of those waiting tensely above.

Keeping back from the edge of the mesa so as not to be spotted by the driver, the outlaws crouched down, nerves strung tight as coiled springs. A lizard scuttled across Chip Flannery's hand before disappearing into a crevice. The unexpected contact strained his already tense nerves.

'Easy, kid,' soothed Santee, noting

the young outlaw's edginess. 'Stick to what we planned and this heist is in the bag.'

Flannery responded with a tight smile.

'Sure thing, boss. Just wanna get on with it, is all.'

As soon as the huffing locomotive had passed, they quickly moved to the rim of the mesa. The first car edged past no more than five feet below, followed closely by the second. They allowed both to pass undisturbed. It was the express car that commanded their sole attention now.

'On my signal we all jump down on to the roof,' shouted Santee, his tight vocals brittle with tension.

The express car clanked by.

Time hung suspended. Then:

'Now!'

In perfect synchronized harmony the three robbers sprang off their rocky perch, landing on the flat central walkway that ran the entire length of the car. Hunkering down automatically, they peered around to ensure that their arrival had not been detected.

All was as it should be. No piercing 'yarrop' from dismayed rail staff disturbed the gentle chugging of the loco as it continued through Fresnal Gap.

Santee didn't need to broadcast any orders. Each man knew his task. Crocker leapt to his feet and hurried quickly to the rear of the car where the all-important brake wheel was located. For one of his bulk, the outlaw was deceptively nimble-footed. He kept a close watch on the open platform below in case the guards became suspicious and decided to investigate.

Meanwhile, Santee had already shimmied down the iron ladder at the front end, followed by Chip Flannery. He peered charily over the side of the covered veranda. Ascertaining that the coupling was of the link-and-pin variety, he visibly relaxed. A relieved whistle filtered from between pursed lips. Most trains by the 1880s had adopted the safer and more reliable knuckle coupler, which would have been hard to disengage from a train on the move.

With Flannery providing much needed additional muscle power, and the pair of them heaving in unison, they had soon extracted the heavy iron link-rod. Almost immediately, the express car began to lose momentum.

The rest of the train rapidly drew away as it picked up speed on the down grade. Santee was well aware that the driver would soon suss out that he had lost one of his cars. But once the train finally came to a standstill, on the far side of Fresnal Gap, the chances of achieving a successful reversal were very low.

Huojin Soo realized something untoward had occurred the moment the express car was released. He was aware of every change, every fickle gesture that might affect the old lady's mood. Engine number 4509 had been his pride and joy for over three years. He treated her as he would a capricious spouse.

So what was it this time?

Soo quickly scanned the gauges for any obvious aberrations. Everything was in order. Indeed 4509 suddenly appeared to have upped her game. The driver stroked his plait of silvery hair, then swung himself out from the cab. Hanging on by his left arm, he peered back up the track.

The sight that met his slanted gaze brought a choked gurgle to the little man's throat. Shocked, he spluttered out a Chinese expletive.

'Scurvy dogs trying to rob train,' he shouted to his fireman. 'Have released express car.'

Quickly recovering from the severe jolt to his nervous system, Soo hauled himself back into the cab and slammed on the brake lever.

Santee was unconcerned about the front end of the train. Wixx and Padora would ensure that any moves to recover the suddenly removed express car would be quickly stymied.

As Crocker applied pressure to the brake wheel a harsh grinding of tortured metal rent the air. Akin to a thousand frightened rats fighting to escape a blazing coop, the effect was immediate. Juddering and shaking in protest, the uncoupled express car rumbled to a halt.

Santee and his sidekick jumped down on to the side of the track. Guns drawn and aimed at the door, they waited. The brakeman soon poked his head out and was quickly driven back inside by a volley of well-placed shots.

'You fellas in there will have gathered by now that this is a hold-up,' shouted the gang boss, injecting a brittle edge into his words. 'All we want are the contents of that safe. And we've got enough dynamite to blow the whole shebang to kingdom come if'n you don't open up.'

He paused to let the import of his declaration sink in. 'You can save yourselves a passel of grief by comin' out now and givin' us free access. Otherwise the whole car gets blown. What's it to be, gents?'

By this time, Hyram Falmer had joined them with the horses.

'That you in there, Chuck?' he called out addressing the brakeman.

A muted response filtered through the wooden walls. Falmer's voice had clearly been recognized. 'I might have known you'd tie in with a bunch of robbers, Falmer,' came back the contemptuous retort. 'Well, you're wasting your goddamned time cos I ain't opening up for nobody.'

'You know this turkey?' broached Santee.

'Sure do,' said Falmer. 'And the bastard means it. A real stubborn critter is Chuck Wesley.'

Santee's brow knitted in thought. Things were not going according to plan. He slammed a balled fist against the side of the car. A throaty growl emerged through clenched teeth. His face turned a deep purple as the frustration of his well-planned caper hung in the balance.

Then an idea struck him. He turned

back to the express car.

'How much does the company pay you, mister?'

'What's that got to do with anything?'

'Well it ain't nearly enough for an employee who's prepared to die for his job,' urged Santee. 'You ready to meet yer maker, Chuck?'

Silence followed.

Santee winked at his associate.

'That's gotten him thinkin',' he muttered with a twisted grin. Then he turned up the pressure a notch. 'What if I was to offer you a cut of the dough?' suggested the gang boss. 'Would that change your mind?'

Another half-minute, then the heavy door swung open and Chuck Wesley stepped out on to the platform. He was a heavy-set dude smartly clad in the company's blue-and-gold livery. Perched on his head was a pillbox cap.

'Now that's what I call a sensible decision.' Santee smirked. He shook his head. 'It's just a darned pity that you couldn't have just opened up in the beginning. As it is, you've made Duke Santee good and mad. And nobody gets away with that.'

The heavy revolver bucked in his fist. Three times, orange flame spat forth. The brakeman staggered back clutching at his shattered chest, a look of disbelief etched across his florid visage. Then he pitched over the low rail at the far side.

Santee blew on the end of his smoking pistol. A fitting end for a skunk who figured to outwit one of his reputation.

'Any more heroes in there?' he called in a grating drawl that intimated their fate should any resistance be encountered. 'If there are, you'd best come out now while the offer to keep breathin' still stands.'

Silence reigned. But only momentarily.

Down the line a flurry of pistol fire, punctuated by the throatier roar of a Greener, rebounded up the cutting.

It appeared that the Chink driver was putting up some resistance. Santee scoffed derisively. The poor dupe was pissing into the wind. Even a newcomer to this game could see that reversing a heavily laden locomotive uphill was like turning lead into gold. He had every confidence in the persuasive abilities of his two henchmen.

Returning his attention to the express car, he hoisted himself up on to the platform and entered the dim interior. A sooty oil lamp provided barely enough light to see the iron-grey strongbox anchored to the floor by four enormous bolts. And it was indeed a mighty specimen. On seeing the giant safe in the flesh, so to speak, it was clear that without the key, dynamite must be the sole means of gaining access to the contents.

And it was obviously going to take all the high explosives they possessed.

After fastening the sticks to the door hinges of the gargantuan money-box Santee secured the fusewire. Falmer had said that a twenty-second length would be sufficient.

'OK boys,' he grinned, addressing the others rather nervously. 'There's gonna be one helluva bang in here. So you'd be advised to get outside and under cover. All we can do now is hope there's enough of the stuff to bust this critter wide open.'

The outlaws needed no second bidding. They hurried outside and scuttled behind a cluster of rocks beside the track. Santee struck a vesta and applied the spluttering flame to the fuse. It immediately hissed and spat, the flame eating its way along the wire in a haze of smoke and sparks.

His eyes bulged. Had he allowed enough time? The blamed fuse was quicker than a roadrunner. Judging it imprudent to hang around, he dashed for the door and jumped off the platform.

'Over here, Major!' yelled Flannery.

Santee dashed towards the gesturing outlaw.

# 5

## Dynamite Daze

An almighty roar lifted the outlaw chief off his feet and slammed him into the ground. One second the express car had been standing on the track, the next it had disintegrated into a million fragments. Debris rained down on to the heads of the cowering robbers. The blue sky had been completely obscured. There was nothing they could do but remain under cover.

Santee hugged the ground. Raised hands protected his head as bits of wood and metal cascaded all around.

It was two minutes before anybody felt confident enough to raise his head. Chip Flannery was the first to cast a wary peeper above the parapet of his rocky sanctuary. The sight he beheld was akin to hell on a bad day. Dense clouds of smoke filled the cutting, making it impossible to ascertain the extent of the damage. His head throbbed, ears ringing with the effect of the huge blast.

He stood up and attempted to pierce the swirling tendrils of smoke. Crocker joined him. Neither spoke. Open-mouthed and staring, they were both stunned into shocked disbelief. Any experience they had acquired regarding the delicate art of safe-blowing was solely through word of mouth.

In slow motion, the haze began to lift, revealing the extent of the damage done to the express car. The iron chassis and bogey wheels were all that was left. The rest was a burnt-out wreck.

And there, emerging from the murky brume were the scorched remnants of the safe. Strips of metal stuck out at all angles like the twisted limbs of some petrified beast. Flames rose from the bed of the car.

Santee lurched to his feet. Luckily he

was uninjured, apart from a few minor cuts and bruises.

'What happened?' he blurted out, although it was becoming patently obvious that far too much dynamite had been used. Fragments of burning paper drifted in the air.

Crocker grabbed hold of one scrap and anxiously peered at it. His fixed gaze and stunned expession was enough to convey the truth of what had occurred minutes before. The money had gone up in smoke along with the car.

A half-mile down the line Charlie Padora's paint mare reared up in fright. The explosion had shaken both outlaws to their very boots. Grim expressions clouded their stony faces.

Wixx cast a wary look at his partner.

'That was a heap more'n any normal explosion,' he exclaimed in trepidation. Smoke billowing from the entrance to the cutting only served to heighten their sense of apprehension.

'Yer sure right there, Laramie,'

concurred Padora seriously. 'This needs investigatin'.'

After jacking a couple of fresh cartridges into the shotgun Padora loosed them at the cab of the mighty locomotive. Lead shot peppered the iron monster. Glass from the shattered side panels rained down over the two railmen cowering inside.

Huojin Soo needed no further motivation to abandon his attempt at reversing back up the grade, although he was more concerned for the damage to his beloved 4509 than to his own health.

'Let's get the poor old gal out of here,' he yelled, urging Crank Tanner, the fireman, to stoke up the boiler.

The panic-stricken, hysterical yelps brought a forced smile to the bleak visage of Laramie Wixx. After dispatching a full cylinder of .45 lead bullets at the chuffing loco he urged his mount back along the track and into the hazy depths of Fresnal Gap. Only the desperate application of rowelled spurs persuaded the apprehensive sorrel to plunge into the dusky chasm.

Padora was quick to follow. Thick frown lines darkening his forehead were sufficient evidence of the horrors he expected to encounter.

'Where's Falmer?' growled Santee dabbing his neckerchief at a streak of blood oozing from his gashed cheek. The esteemed grey uniform, covered in dirt and dust, went unheeded.

No reply was forthcoming.

Only after Wixx and Padora had arrived was the mystery solved. The younger outlaw pointed to a spike of iron poking from behind a boulder.

'Seems like Falmer chose the wrong place to shelter.' The comment was issued in a less than sympathetic tone. The ex-railroader was no great loss. He had been tolerated solely on account of his inside knowledge.

Santee shuffled across, still suffering the aftereffects of the massive blast. He fastened a cool eye on to the splayed-out body now skewered to the hard ground by the lethal shard of metal. The gang leader's reaction was even less generous. He spat contemptuously on the the bleeding corpse.

'If that hadn't done fer him, then I surely would have,' he ventured with a snarl. 'The little weasel should never have persuaded me to use dynamite.'

Anger and frustration at having his plans thwarted came bubbling to the surface. Santee palmed his revolver and pumped a full load into the grisly corpse. The starkly brutal act didn't make him feel one jot better. And the sight of charred greenbacks drifting in the air only served to depress him even further.

It was the pragmatic Wixx who brought a sense of practicality to the bizarre proceedings.

Clarity of thought was needed. And that meant getting away from Fresnal Gap and the blackened hulk of the Flagstaff Flyer express car lickety split. They could analyse what had gone wrong once they were back at Buffalo

Wash, safe from the investigation that would undoubtedly follow.

Snapping and barking like an injured puma, Santee was in no mood for practical advice. Nonetheless, he was astute enough to savvy that hanging around the confines of the Gap and feeling sorry for himself would achieve nothing.

And Flagstaff was only twenty miles down the line. Better to slip away and lick his wounds in safety.

'OK, boys,' he muttered, heaving his tired frame into the saddle, 'No sense cryin' over spilt milk. Let's hit the trail.'

★   ★   ★

It was late evening before the gang reached Buffalo Wash. Santee had judged it prudent to avoid the main trail by detouring through Sedona Canyon and over Dead Horse Pass. The less travelled northern trail was rougher and more tortuous but it had the advantage of avoiding any settlements. For that fact alone it was little used.

Streaks of purple and gold were being swallowed up by the dense mantle of the night sky. Sharply honed peaks of the surrounding Trinity Mountains stood proud against the western horizon as the sorry group of riders reined in.

The log cabin occupied by the gang was an abandoned line shack. Surrounded by stands of dwarf willow some fifty yards back from the chattering waters of the Wash, it was hidden from casual view, virtually undetectable by any interlopers passing down the valley. In consequence it made for the perfect hideout.

'Who's on chow detail?' enquired a hungry Crocker.

'Might have known T-Bone would be thinkin' of his stomach,' hallooed Chip Flannery. The two outlaws were riding abreast. In appearance, they were as different as sheep from longhorns.

The others nodded in understanding.

Apart from Duke Santee, all gang members were on a cooking roster, due to the fact that nobody had volunteered for the job. Cooking was definitely a specialist occupation. So it stood to reason that the quality of meals varied accordingly.

Charlie Padora always stuck to son-of-a-gun stew which he had learned how to concoct while on trail drives back in the early '70s. Whereas T-Bone Crocker would have lived on nothing but thick steaks if he had the chance.

'He ain't sayin' but I'm darned certain it's the guy from Wyoming's turn for apron chores,' Flannery scoffed, a caustic leer pasted across his smoothly youthful complexion.

As one, all eyes slewed in Wixx's direction. The stocky gunman's shoulders lifted in a resigned shrug. There was no escaping chow duty.

Flannery had resisted once and been thrown into the Wash by the others. It had been a particularly cold January with ice coating the surface of the river. They had not let him out for an hour. It was not a penalty he would wish to repeat.

While Wixx shambled off to organize the evening meal each man saw to the feeding and watering of his own mount. Santee disappeared into the back room, which he had commandeered for his own use. He was in no mood for socializing. When it was ready, he ate his meal, washed down with a jug of Padora's patent moonshine.

Not before the midnight hour had passed did he finally emerge. And then only at the behest of Charlie Padora.

The old guy had been reading a copy of the *Flagstaff Herald* that had somehow escaped the express car conflagration.

The feature was a small paragraph listed under *STOP PRESS* on the back page. Nearly passed over, it was the lead title that had caught Padora's attention.

## DYNAMITE MAN GETS A TEN STRETCH FOR ATTEMPTED MURDER

Lee Jago, a construction engineer with the Standard Pacific Railroad, was today convicted of blowing up a residential Pullman car. He had mistakenly assumed that his boss, Bradley Straker, was inside asleep. Luckily, the manager had been called away on business the night before.

Apprehended by foreman Rafe Boondock at the scene of the brutal crime, Jago made no attempt to deny his actions. His assertion was that it had been in retaliation for his boss's heartless disregard for the lives of the Chinese workers in his employ. Fifteen coolies had died in a tunnel being cut through the Weaver Mountains. Straker forcefully denied any negligence on his part.

A guilty verdict was inevitable. The felon will be taken under guard overland to the Yuma State Prison on Tuesday July 15, 1880, there to begin a sentence of ten years' hard labour.

A full transcript of the trial conducted by Judge Henry Tomlin will be in tomorrow's edition of the *Herald*.

Padora read the article three times before the significance of its content struck him like a raging tornado. Here could be the answer to their dilemma.

'Take a peek at this, Major,' Padora urged. Unable to contain his excitement, he handed the paper across the table, jabbing a finger at the vital press report.

'What's so darned important that it can't wait until morning?' muttered Santee, waving the jug at the old reprobate.

'Might be we could get ourselves a jasper who knows his dynamite.'

Padora's eagerness caught the attention of the others, who now gathered round. Santee grabbed a hold of the paper and proceeded to read the report.

Crocker couldn't hold back his impatience.

'What's it say then, boss?' he urged. 'Readin' ain't my strong point.'

The gang leader ignored the fervid appeals. Carefully he scanned the contents of the article, digesting their significance with care and deliberation. He then lit up a cigar before responding.

'Seems like you could have a point, Shotgun,' he praised the old outlaw, slapping him on the back. 'So here it is, boys,' he said, addressing the others. Settling back in his seat, he then read the article out aloud.

When he had finished Flannery asked, 'What date is it now?'

Santee fished out a large gold-plated watch from his vest pocket and thumbed open the cover. 'According to my Hunter Excelsior, we have just entered Sunday July thirteen.'

'Which means,' iterated a thunderstruck T-Bone Crocker, 'that we only have one day to plan this snatch.' Snickering like a petulant peacock he preened, 'I might not be good with the words, fellas, but my numbers ain't a problem.'

'You sure are right there, T-Bone,' Flannery chuckled, winking at the others while trying to keep a straight face. Muted guffaws were aimed at the corpulent outlaw.

But Crocker was too busy finishing off the last of the stew left by Flannery to notice the joshing at his expense. Nothing ever came between Crocker and his stomach.

As ever, it was Wixx who brought the talk back to the issue in hand.

'If this jigger is being taken to Yuma by prison wagon,' he propounded, 'they'll take the trail through Sedona Canyon, which makes it easier for us.'

'I wouldn't be so darned certain about that,' cautioned a wistful Charlie Padora scratching at the few grey hairs that still graced his round pate.

Santee pricked up his ears.

'What yuh on about, Charlie?' he questioned.

'Served two years in the state prison down at Bisbee near the Mex border.' Padora shook his head as the harsh memory resurfaced. 'And all for snuffin' out a crooked gambler. Bastard was dealin' from the bottom of the deck. At least I got me a sympathetic judge. After the trial, me and five other dudes were taken there in one of them war wagons.' The old guy rolled his eyes. 'Trust me when I tell yuh, boys. That sure weren't no Sunday picnic.'

The younger members of the gang listened intently, mouths agape. None of them had ever set foot inside a town hoosegow, let alone the state pen. Such was the advantage of being in with Duke Santee.

'What was it like?' from a spellbound Chip Flannery.

'Them warders were just itchin' to use their whips on us poor saps at the slightest pretext. Got me the scars to prove it.' He was about to lift up his shirt when Santee interrupted him.

'Just stick to the point, Charlie,' he rapped spitting a lump of pork gristle into the smoking hearth. 'We ain't got time for your sob story.'

The old convict's seamed visage crinkled at the sour rebuke. But Santee's stony regard stilled any reciprocating comment. Hitching up his baggy trousers, Padora fired up a smelly corn cob and sucked hard before resuming.

'Them there war wagons have three guards,' he said. 'Two ridin' up front armed with riot guns, and another perched on the back behind a reinforced shield.'

'We oughta be capable of takin' out three guards,' opined Crocker through a mouthful of apple dumpling.

'If you'd let me finish, jughead,' admonished Padora, glaring at his confederate, 'I was about to add that two other guards ride ahead to warn of just the sort of bust-out that we're after performin'.'

'Hmm,' murmured Santee. He stood up and paced the room. 'We need to separate those point riders from the wagon so's they can't give no back-up.'

In these equivocal situations, a rich

Havana cigar had always helped him come up with a suitable plan in the past. This time was no exception. After five minutes, during which time a tense silence held the others in a mesmeric grip, the gang leader clicked his fingers, breaking the spell.

'And I know just the place for the perfect bust.'

A broad grin spread across his grizzled countenance. Dark eyes glittered as the plan took shape in his shifty agile mind. Now it was merely a question of sorting out the details.

# 6

## The Devil's Switchblade

In keeping with his regular practice, Duke Santee led his men off from the Buffalo Wash hideout at an early hour so they would be in position by sun-up the following morning. Trekking back over Dead Horse Pass, they descended a steep zigzagging trail.

On their right the unmistakable upsurge of yellow sandstone known as Coffee Pot Mesa stood etched against a blue backdrop. Capped by a wedge of cotton wool cumulus, it gave the impression that the beverage was just waiting to be poured by some giant hand. Whenever he came this way, Chip Flannery was always transfixed by this awesome display of nature's bounty. Although he would never have admitted as much to the others.

As they descended the hazardous Sidewinder in single file, a cooling breeze helped to alleviate the incessant beating down of the high-riding sun.

They reached the Devil's Switchblade around late afternoon, affording Santee sufficient time to investigate the arena of action.

The Blade was a constricted gash in the rugged mountain fastness of the Junipers where Crazy Lion Creek had exploited a weakness in the bedrock. A narrow chasm with vertical rock walls on either side, it was barely more than thirty feet across. Bursting forth from the hard grasp of the rocky enclave some two miles downstream, the swirling waters thereafter merged with the Verde River, meandering south to swell the mighty Colorado near Yuma.

At its narrowest point a bridge had been constructed across the fissure. Thick cables of rope anchored the flimsy structure which was suspended precariously above the thrashing maelstrom below. Traffic crossing the bridge at anything more than a snail's pace caused it to sway alarmingly.

This was where Santee intended to isolate the two point guards on the far side by cutting the rope stanchions and sending the ungainly pile plunging into the chasm. In the event of the guards managing to fire off warning shots to alert their confederates in charge of the prison wagon, he intended placing men in a strategic position to forestall any attempted withdrawal.

The wagon would then effectively be trapped between the Devil and Hades.

It was a sound plan. As with all such daring schemes, success depended upon the element of surprise. Each gang member would need to carry out his part of the operation with disciplined precision.

Over mugs of strong Arbuckles, they gathered round a campfire. It was set well back off the main trail up a blind draw hidden from the prying eyes of any unwelcome travellers. Santee instructed each man as to his part in the forthcoming action, emphasizing the need for exactitude.

There would be no heroics. No veering away from the blueprint he had devised, unless things went awry. Then it would be every man for himself.

First priority was to cut the cables, just enough to enable the advance guards to cross without bringing the structure tumbling down. A couple of swift hacks with an axe would then finish the job, thus preventing any retaliatory manoeuvres.

'Boy, that's some fierce piece of water,' commented an overawed Chip Flannery, raising his voice above the level of the thunderous clamour below. 'No way can those guards get back once the bridge collapses.'

Santee smiled, his gnarled features crinkling up like old shoe leather as he handed an axe to the young hardcase.

'Make sure you only chop halfway through each cable', he stressed, wagging an admonitory finger in the kid's face. 'We don't wanna give them jiggers any chance to turn the tables on us.'

Wixx and Padora had already sniffed out a suitable place of concealment back up the trail to trap the prison wagon inside the canyon.

'I noticed some juniper trees back there,' said Wixx, grabbing hold of a second axe. 'We can chop down a few. Soon as the wagons have passed, Shotgun and me can then toss them across the trail.'

'Good thinkin', Laramie,' commended Santee.

'What happens if any other riders happen along?' enquired Crocker who was spit-roasting a rabbit.

'Too bad for them.' The gang boss shrugged. 'They shoulda chose a different route.' His black eyes glazed over, narrowing to thin slits. 'So we deal with 'em . . . on a permanent basis.' His hand made a cutting motion across his throat. There was no mistaking the terminal gesture.

Wixx grinned. That was the sort of talk he relished.

★　★　★

Crocker was up before first light. No way was he missing out on breakfast. The redolent aroma of frying bacon and freshly brewed coffee soon roused the others. After quickly shovelling down his own meal, Santee was soon toeing sand over the fire just as the false dawn was breaking over the eastern rim of the junipers. He was anxious that everyone should be in position by sun-up.

They had no way of knowing when the prison wagon would arrive at the Devil's Switchblade. It might be a long wait.

'On your way, Laramie,' ordered Santee.

The young outlaw stubbed out his cigarillo and trotted across to his cayuse, leaping acrobatically into the saddle from the rear.

'Ain't you comin', Shotgun?' He grinned down at his sidekick.

The old guy raised a jaundiced

eyebrow, sniggering as he ambled casually over to his own mount. 'You'd do well to recall the tale about the hare and the tortoise,' he cautioned while hoisting his creaking frame into the saddle. 'Or you might come to a sticky end. That's what I say.'

Not having heard tell of the renowned fable, Wixx gave him a puzzled frown before spurring off up the trail.

It was mid-morning when the steady drum of approaching hoofbeats impinged upon Duke Santee's attuned ears. His back stiffened. Rifle at the ready, he quickly checked the loadings of his handgun. On the far side of the trail he noted Flannery's raised arm indicating that he also had picked up on the tell-tale sign.

In less than a minute, two riders appeared. They reined up beside the ravine, studying the ungainly structure that had to be negotiated. Santee held his breath, praying that they didn't look down and notice the partly severed cables. Taut nerves made him clutch the butt of his rifle, knuckles white as an artic fox.

Beside him, the rasping breath of T-Bone Crocker grated alarmingly.

The two guards exchanged a few words then gingerly nudged their mounts forward on to the roped slats of the swaying structure.

At that moment the deep rumble of the approaching prison wagon echoed down the canyon.

The moment of truth had arrived.

★   ★   ★

Gaunt-faced and clad in the regulation convict uniforms of horizontal stripes, five men occupied the interior of the prison wagon. All were securely manacled with leg-irons and handcuffs fixed to a central post in the middle of the floor. Two small windows on either side were heavily barred and the only door was fastened by three large padlocks.

Up front was a driver and guard,

while seated on a bench to the rear sat a third. They all wore peaked caps emblazoned with the Yuma badge and were armed with Colt pistols and the latest Winchester repeaters. Only the most foolhardy desperado would attempt to liberate the inmates.

They had not reckoned with the wily machinations of Major Duke Santee.

Inside the wagon a single bucket of water had to suffice until the detachment reached Prescott. Only then would the prisoners be allowed to stretch their legs and attend to calls of nature. They had come less than halfway and already the bucket was almost empty. With men being crammed into such a tiny space, the heat was intense. All of the convicts were sweating freely, and the smell inside the wagon was appalling.

Their newly shaven heads drooped on to the rough serge tunics. Brains had been stunned into submission at the thought of spending the next few years in Arizona's most notorious prison.

Three of the men had been found guilty of murder in the course of felonious activities associated with bank robberies and hold-ups.

Another was there for shooting his wife's lover after catching them in a compromising situation, then slitting the woman's throat. He had given himself up the next day. Under the circumstances, the judge had been lenient and sentenced the man to only five years.

It was the fifth convict who was the enigma.

Railroad engineer Lee Jago was no robber. Neither was he a spurned husband. His was a case of what he considered to be justifiable retribution for a wrong committed by his superiors. No such case had ever previously been brought before the Flagstaff law courts.

The directors of the Standard Pacific Railroad carried substantial influence and pressed for the maximum sentence. Even though Jago had pleaded guilty, the fact that he expressed no remorse for his actions, neither had he put forward any extenuating circumstances, meant that a heavy sentence was imposed with no chance of parole. Judge Tomlin had indicated that only through pure chance had the sentence imposed been custodial rather than a visit by the state hangman.

The engineer now had ample time to brood over the events that had brought a promising career crashing down about his ears. Glassy eyes stared blankly out of the window, seeing nothing.

Had the salving of his conscience been worth the sacrifice? The noble gesture versus liberty. Only time would tell. And he had plenty of that.

# 7

## Rescue

Lee stared out of the barred window of the stifling prison wagon. An involuntary hand strayed to the bloodstained bandage swathing his head. The fact that he was still alive came as little consolation. All he could see were the delicate features of his wife sitting forlorn and alone in the courtroom. Chuan Li's long black hair framed an oval face of exquisite beauty that registered the intense pain the judge's harsh sentencing had caused her.

As he held his head in his hands, an almost suppressed moan escaped from between the condemned engineer's tight lips.

The other convicts squinted at the thoughtful half-caste. The three bank robbers were old hands at this game.

They knew the score and how to deal with it.

'Don't whine and sob, if'n yuh cain't do the job,' one of them scoffed. Jeering guffaws followed the hard-boiled witticism.

'Maybe he's comin' to realize that crime don't pay,' suggested a thin-faced dude.

'It does if'n yuh gets away with it,' sighed his partner ruefully.

'Now why didn't we think of that before tryin' to rob that bank in Flagstaff,' breezed a thick-set man to his right.

'You shoulda checked it out for armed guards before we blundered in there like greenhorns.' The grumbled riposte was aimed at the heavy-set bearded outlaw who had been the leader of the sorry trio.

'And you oughta keep that big trap of your'n shut fast if'n yuh wanna reach Yuma in one piece,' snarled the big dude, rattling his chains impotently.

'Keep that noise down,' came the

brusque command from one of the guards. 'Else I'll be givin' this bullwhip some exercise.' A sharp crack from the fifteen-foot braid cut through the fetid air.

The threat of a brutal rawhide scourging was enough to bring the burgeoning squabble to an abrupt end.

During the dispute, the spurned husband had listened in amused silence. He had friends on the Yuma prison board and enough dough stashed away to smooth out his time at the infamous prison.

But all this repartee passed Lee Jago by completely. He wasn't even listening.

All he could think of was that he had allowed unbridled emotions rather than his head to rule his actions. And this was where it had led him. Chuan Li had said she would wait for him. But how could he expect such a graceful and comely blossom to sit around for ten years?

There would be no dearth of eager suitors willing to take his place in the marital bed. Gloom and despondency settled over his bowed head at the thought of his lovely wife succumbing to such lecherous fumblings.

The only saving grace in this whole sorry affair was that Straker had cheated the grim reaper, thus saving Lee from being labelled a killer. But the unscrupulous manager had not escaped all reprisal. Indeed he had paid a heavy price for his skulduggery.

Word had trickled down the prison grapevine that publicity generated by the trial had led to his nefarious activities being brought to the attention of the company bosses. As a result he had been summarily dismissed.

This, however, was of little concern to the engineer who now had endless days of brutal drudgery ahead during which to repent his actions.

★　★　★

Once the pair of guards had reached the halfway point across the bridge, Chip Flannery slipped out from behind a boulder and began vigorously chopping at the thick hemp cables. The noise instantly alerted the guards. Quick on the uptake they immediately spurred their mounts to the far side leaping the last few feet before the ungainly structure disintegrated.

One of the horses, less agile than its mate flopped on the edge of the ravine. Its hind legs thrashed wildly, trying to gain some degree of purchase on the crumbling lip.

'Grab my hand, Ben!' yelled the first guard leaping from his cayuse and reaching out to his partner.

It was a futile endeavour. The whinnying beast slid over the edge in a welter of flailing legs. Rider and horse plunged into the turbulent maelstrom of the Devil's Switchblade and were instantly swallowed up by the river's insatiable appetite.

Bullets whined and buzzed around the head of the surviving guard, one of which struck down his horse. Realizing the grim reality of his situation, Buck

Rogers dived for cover behind the twitching carcass. More bullets thumped into the soft flesh.

It was obvious that an attempt was being made to free the prisoners.

But at least he still had access to his rifle, which he dragged from its boot. Jacking a shell up the spout, Rogers peered round the side of the dead horse. One of the bushwhackers was hustling across open ground on the far side. He clearly figured that both of the lead guards had been neutralized.

A big mistake!

Santee had ordered Crocker to move back up the canyon once the bridge had gone, in readiness for the arrival of the prison wagon. He had observed the surviving guard taking cover and knew he was still a threat that needed removing.

Never the fastest of movers, Crocker's progress to the far side of the canyon seemed more lethargic than usual.

'Move yer lazy ass, T-Bone!' yelled the gang leader.

The stocky outlaw acknowledged the gruff retort with a less than polite gesture. It was to be his last.

All it took was a single deep-throated roar from a Sharps Big 50 to cut the lumbering hardcase down. Throwing up his arms, Crocker tumbled forward into the dust and lay still.

Santee growled, muttering a few lurid imprecations under his breath. But he wasted no time in pointless regret on the sudden loss of a long-serving sidekick. He grabbed up the Winchester and loosed off a flurry of accurate rifle fire which kept the remaining guard pinned down behind his dead cayuse.

This brief distraction provided Santee with the opportunity to move back up the canyon. At the same time he signalled for Flannery to do likwise on the far side. Sufficient cover was afforded by the broad spread of many boulders and a scattering of thorny mesquite.

As he despaired of his dire situation Jago's clouded brain was enveloped in a fresh wave of anguish. The engineer was so wrapped up in his own misery that he failed to heed the rattle of gunfire echoing down the canyon. The sharp cracks from long guns was amplifed by the steep, sometimes almost vertical walls of the narrowing gorge.

'What was that?' enquired one of the prisoners eagerly peering out of the window.

'Sounds like gunfire to me,' replied his companion.

'Could be this guy's moll tryin' to bust him out,' chuckled the bearded erstwhile leader of the gang. Nervous laughter followed. Any lingering resentment between the outlaws was now forgotten as this new diversion promised a possible end to their imprisonment. Necks strained in an effort to see what was happening beyond the confines of their mobile prison.

★  ★  ★

The driver of the wagon hollered at the team of six as he hauled back on the leathers, bringing the ungainly vehicle to a stumbling halt. Swivelling round, he soon realized that the wagon was effectively trapped. Two men were flinging cut-down trees across the trail.

A sharp pistol report rang out as one of them decided to up the stakes.

It was followed by a choking cry of pain.

'Ugh!' gasped the rear shotgun rider, slumping forward. 'I've been hit.' A second shot followed. It finished off the guard whose dead body lay splayed out across the metal shield that had failed miserably to protect him.

'Now that you fellas know we mean business,' snarled Laramie Wixx, swinging his revolver to cover the two front guards, 'you'd be well advised to hoist yer mitts. Any tricks and my buddy here will cut yuh both in half.'

Shotgun Charlie stepped out from

behind a boulder and wagged his sawn-off at the gaping pair of guards.

'You heard the man,' barked Duke Santee. 'Good work, boys,' he added joining Wixx and Padora. 'Them front runners ain't gonna be causin' no trouble. So we got no need to rush things.'

'They got old T-Bone, though,' lamented the downcast Flannery. 'The poor sap just wasn't fast enough on his pins.'

'Is he dead?' croaked an unsettled Charlie Padora.

Flannery responded with a brief nod.

The driver snorted, a coarse guffaw his instinctive reaction.

'One less thieving skunk to sample Yuma's hospitality.'

It was not a remark likely to endear him to the ageing outlaw.

A low growl rattled in the old guy's throat. The guzzling Crocker had been his best pal. They had ridden together since long before joining up with Duke Santee's bunch of rough riders. His rheumy eyes narrowed to thin slits, an ugly slash cutting across his weathered features.

A double click cut through the air as both shotgun hammers snapped back. He stepped forward.

In choice words uttered barely above a whisper he hissed, 'You oughtn't to have said that, mister.'

The sneering chortle was the wrong response.

*Crash!*

A single roar from both barrels lifted the driver off his seat, flinging him like a discarded rag doll, over the side of the wagon. Blood poured from the huge hole in his shattered chest cavity, staining the desert sand a dun hue. Overhead, an interested buzzard circled in anticipation of this unexpected repast. At ground level two coyotes howled in competition for the rare treat.

'D-don't sh-shoot!' burbled the remaining guard. Arms clutching at the heavens he slithered down off the driving seat, sweat glistening on a twitching brow.

His anxious gaze flitted between the hard faces staring back. 'I ain't gonna cause no fracas boys,' he stammered. 'Just take whoever it is you're after.'

'That's just what we aim to do,' chuckled a gleeful Duke Santee. 'Ain't that so, boys?'

'Sure is,' laughed Chip Flannery. The others joined in the hilarity, including those inside the wagon, who suddenly realized that their incarceration had come to a sudden and welcome end. Only Charlie Padora remained tight-lipped. This was no celebration for him. The old reprobate ambled disconsolately back up the trail to attend to his *amigo*.

'Is there a railroad engineer among you jaspers?' asked Santee, opening the door of the wagon with keys he had obtained from the only too helpful surviving guard.

Lee Jago was still staring out of the far window, seemingly unaware of the brutal drama recently played out around him.

'This is the guy you want,' offered the rejected husband, jabbing a thumb at the recumbent form in the corner. 'But he ain't had much to say for hisself.'

'We want his railroad knowledge, not some sharp-tongued smart-ass,' snapped Santee. He unlocked the chain that secured the engineer to the central holding post. 'Out yuh come, fella. We got need of your talents.'

A nudge from the husband jerked Lee from his internal reveries. Without thinking he stood and shambled out of the wagon, suddenly realizing that he was free. A wave of hope lit up his jaundiced face, a rejuvenated aspiration that he might now be able to put things right with his wife.

But the shining beacon in his brain was snuffed before it had time to grow. What did these men want with him?

Clearly they had not gone to all this trouble for his benefit alone. Nonetheless, being free was a start. The future could not be any worse than a ten stretch in Yuma.

'Take your boots off,' Santee ordered the guard.

'What?'

'You heard the boss,' snarled Wixx. He jabbed the snout of his revolver into the guy's back.

The guard quickly did as requested, watching as his footwear was chopped into bits by the grinning Wixx.

'Now git walkin'.'

'It's twenty miles back to Flagstaff,' moaned the guard.

'Then you best get a shift on,' chortled Flannery. He fired a full load of bullets into the sand around the bare feet of the worried guard.

Leaping about like a Mexican jumping bean, the startled guy quickly hustled off in a northerly direction, followed by more well-placed shots that had him dancing a merry jig, much to the amusement of all those who were watching.

Once the man had disappeared from view, Santee pushed Lee towards the spare horse brought specifically for his use. The others followed behind and mounted up.

'Hey, mister,' called out one of the prisoners who were still shackled inside the prison wagon. 'What about us? Ain't yer gonna set us free?' There was deep concern in his trembling enquiry as he suddenly realized that they were about to be abandoned.

Santee gave the jigger a puzzled frown then scratched his bearded chin in thought. The remaining prisoners waited on tenterhooks, hanging on the outlaw leader's decision.

A smile cracked the granite profile.

'Just joshin', boys.' He grinned. 'Catch!'

The heavy set of keys flew threw the air. They clattered against the open door then tumbled into the sand. One prisoner stretched out an arm to retrieve them. But they were just out of reach. His eyes widened in alarm, mouth agape.

The Rough Riders laughed at the unexpected predicament then spurred their mounts back up the trail, Lee Jago penned into the middle of the group. Riding past the makeshift grave of T-Bone Crocker prompted Old Shotgun to comment, 'Yuh ain't gonna leave them fellas stranded back there are yuh, Major?'

'Why not?' came back the acid retort.

'Don't seem right somehow. To our own kind.'

'Goin' soft in yer old age, Charlie?' Chip Flannery laughed.

'What d'yuh say, boss?' pressed Padora, ignoring the jibe.

Santee considered the suggestion then replied with a shrug, 'Go on then, if'n you've a mind.'

'It's the right thing to do,' answered Padora. He swung his paint round.

\* \* \*

It was early evening when the group of riders headed up Buffalo Wash to the welcome if spartan comforts of their hideout. Not until supper was finished and they were relaxing in the company of some red label whiskey did the gang leader inform his guest what was required of him.

Once he had been apprised of the gang's intentions, Lee had little hesitation in agreeing to their demands on his expertise — not that he was given any choice. But putting one over on the Standard Pacific railroad came a poor second on his list of priorities now that he was free.

First off, he wanted to get word to his wife.

That was not going to be as simple as he had originally thought. Duke Santee had no intention of allowing his new recruit any freedom of movement until the job had been successfully pulled.

Lee would have to bide his time.

Next morning, over a breakfast of refried beans and tortillas courtesy of Charlie Padora, Santee closely questioned Jago as to his professional qualifications. Curiosity from the rest of the gang soon found Lee pouring out an account of the events leading to his incarceration.

It was a sad tale. But Lee felt better for having unburdened himself.

'We need you to give us the best place to stop the train and blow the safe in the Flyer's express car.' The gang boss skipped over his unfamiliarity with the effective use of explosives, emphasizing the need to obtain the greenbacks without destroying them. A story was concocted regarding an incompetent gang who had used too much dynamite and come away from the heist empty-handed.

Lee struggled to maintain a straight face, strongly suspecting the truth of the matter. The inept foul-up by an unnamed gang of outlaws had spread rapidly throughout the railroad camps. And the company had not been slow in making the appropriate changes to ensure it didn't happen again.

He voiced his doubts with care.

'Robbing a Standard Pacific train is not an operation I would plan in a hurry.'

Santee frowned, pushing an unruly lock of greasy hair beneath his hat. This was not what he wanted to hear.

'What's the darned problem?' he snapped waspishly. 'It worked last time.'

'The company has tightened up security,' replied Lee, keeping a watchful eye on the the outlaw's reaction. 'Extra guards are now posted on all trains hauling valuable freight, especially where payrolls are involved.'

Wixx let out a snort of irritation. 'So what we gonna do? Just give up?'

'That sure ain't an option,' rasped Santee, spearing his confederate with a demonic glare. 'This guy will earn his freedom, or we'll throw him back to the wolves.' He turned to the dynamite expert. 'Ball's in your court, fella,' he commented with a nonchalant shrug. 'Find a way for us to lift the dough, or . . . ' He tapped the revolver on his hip.

Lee didn't need to be told of the consequences should he fail to deliver.

'I need time to think this out,' came

back the measured rejoinder. He stood and made for the door.

'Where yuh goin?' rapped Wixx, slapping leather.

'How do you expect me to conjure up a plan of action with you guys breathing down my neck?' Lee snapped back, ignoring the palmed revolver. 'I need space to think after being cooped up in that blamed prison wagon.'

'What's yer handle, anyway?' asked Padora.

'And where'd yuh hail from?' added Santee, crinkling his mischievous eyes. He was curious about this oddball. He certainly was not from round these parts. Or any of the south-west territories for that matter.

'The name's Lee Jago. And if you're wondering about my accent, it's a mixture of French and Scottish.'

The lie tripped off Lee's tongue with the slickness of a travelling drummer. He had perfected it over the years to conceal his true origins. Any hint of his Chinese ancestry would only encourage derision and scorn from this bunch of hard-bitten gunmen. Maybe even a bullet in the back.

Without waiting for a reaction, Lee left the cabin and wandered down to the shallow waters of Buffalo Wash.

Santee turned to Chip Flannery once the engineer had left.

'Keep an eye on him,' he rapped. 'Make sure he don't try to escape.' Then with an evil snort, he added, 'Once he's delivered the goods into our hands, Laramie here can exercise that gun hand of his.'

Brittle laughter followed this revelation.

Even though Santee had promised him an equal cut of the loot, Lee didn't trust the outlaw boss. Nor did he trust any of his hard-boiled sidekicks, who wouldn't bat an eye over another dead body.

The engineer shivered.

Had he jumped from the frying pan into the fire?

Maybe.

But if he could somehow turn the tables on this bunch of misfits and return the loot to the company, perhaps he could get a reduced sentence. Even earn himself a reprieve.

# 8

## Safe as Egg Shells

It was Friday afternoon.

The Rough Riders were camped in a closed-off gulch some three miles to the south west of Flagstaff. Chip Flannery was saddling his horse. He had been assigned the job of visiting the town and locating the head office of the Standard Pacific Railroad. Jago had described it as being a two-storey brick building located at the northern end of Kaibab Street close to the rail depot.

Adjoining it was a dry-goods store.

Lee had made a solid case for robbing the company office because that was where all funds were kept. Not only payrolls for the surrounding mine operations, but railroad cash as well.

The plan was to break into the store after it closed for business on Saturday evening. They would then have all that night and the following Sunday to break through the wall into the railroad office where the safe was located.

Saturday was always the rowdiest time of the week in any frontier town. The raucous hell-raising would effectively hide noise made during the robbery.

'We'll need at least three mattresses to muffle the sound of the dynamite,' Lee informed the listening outlaws. They hung on his every word, knowing the engineer was their ticket to the easy life, at least for a few months, once the company safe had been successfully blown.

'What are they for?' enquired a perplexed Flannery.

Wixx gave his naïve sidekick a look of withering scorn.

'To muffle the sound of the dynamite, knucklehead,' he mocked.

'It's lucky for us that the mercantile next to the office sells them,' Lee continued, knowing he now had the whip hand. 'All we have to do is break in after dark and carry the goods upstairs to the stockroom adjoining the company office.'

'And a store like that will have jemmies and crowbars for bustin' through the brick wall,' observed the astute Wixx.

Lee nodded before addressing Flannery. 'You'll need to go into the store and find out all you can about times of business.'

'And check out whether the place has a guard,' rapped Santee, wanting to add his weight to the discussion. 'And whether the law has a regular beat.'

★   ★   ★

On the following evening, Saturday, the gang led by Major Duke Santee arrived in Flagstaff. Shadows of approaching night were settling over the town. The last traces of a cloudless day were fast disappearing behind the scalloped moulding of the Weaver Mountains.

Yet, even at this hour, the wide main street was a bustle of chaotic activity, with laden wagons and mule trains clamouring for space. The crack of bullwhips split the air alongside gruff orders from the muleskinners. A flash rainstorm during the day had turned the dusty street into a quagmire of clinging mud. Deep ruts were filled with water, slowing progress down to that of a reluctant shotgun bridegroom.

The difficult conditions were a blessing in disguise.

Five riders nudging their mounts down one side of the thoroughfare in single file attracted no unwelcome attention. Just another bunch of miners hoping to strike it rich in the territory's newly opened goldfields.

An uproarious cacophony from jangling pianos and twanging banjos emanated from the numerous saloons lining Main Street. Gaudy signboards such as those of the Pink Flamingo, Silver Rail, Lost Dutchman and Red Rooster enticed drinkers and gamblers through their open doors.

Had any eagle-eyed bystander taken the trouble he might have noticed that one of the riders was not wearing a holstered pistol, nor was the guy in possession of a booted long gun. Lee Jago was being kept on a tight rein.

Halfway down the street Santee noticed his scout on the far side at the entrance to an alley between a saloon and a drapery store.

'There's Flannery.'

He pointed to the gesturing figure, then nudged his mount gingerly out into the flow of traffic. Crossing the street was a hazardous undertaking which drew forth numerous lurid curses from the steady flow of teamsters passing by.

Once they had negotiated the perilous obstacle course, the riders dismounted and tied their mounts to a free hitch rail. A drink was called for so that Flannery could impart what he had learned from his brief reconnaissance. One at a time, to avoid attracting any unwanted attention, they entered the Barking Mad saloon.

It was well named. The place was heaving. A crazy banjo player jigging about on a table in the middle of the room vigorously stamped his boots in time to the music. He was accompanied by an equally outrageous Mexican dancer cavorting wildly on the adjacent table, her twirling skirts revealing more than enough to entertain the ogling patrons.

Flannery paused, his youthful eyes wide and staring, mouth slavering as he took in the erotic display.

'Keep that pecker of your'n in check until this is all over, kid,' hissed Santee, digging Flannery in the ribs. 'We got work to do.'

But nobody paid the hard-faced outlaws any attention.

After procuring a bottle of whiskey, Santee wound a tortuous path through the heaving throng of revellers to a free table at the back of the dimly lit room. The bottle was passed round, each man slaking his thirst.

'So what's the griff?' enquired Santee without preamble. 'Is this caper on?'

'Sure is, boss,' enthused the eager young tearaway. 'Breaking into the store will be kid's stuff. Being Saturday, the owner shut up shop early. And he won't be reopening until eight o'clock on Monday morning.'

'Plenty of time for what we want,' observed Padora, taking another hefty slug from the now half-empty bottle.

'There'll be no more of that stuff until the job's finished.' Santee grabbed the bottle and stuck it inside his grey coat.

'And that's not all,' continued Flannery, pushing out a taut laugh. 'The jasper has left the back window open. All we have to do is climb through and we're inside. No need for any noisy break-in.'

'Apart from bustin' through the brick wall into the rail office,' added the ever-practical Laramie Wixx.

'We'll wait until after midnight before

gettin' started,' said Santee.

'How about us havin' a meal?' suggested Flannery. 'My stomach's rumblin' somep'n awful.'

'That's old Charlie's cookin' for yuh,' commented Wixx.

The general laughter helped ease the atmosphere.

'And I know just the place,' offered the engineer. 'Ma Dingle's All American Diner serves the biggest steaks in Arizona.'

'That'll do fer me.' Santee pushed back his chair and headed for the door. 'And we'll need plenty of strong black coffee if it's gonna be an all-nighter,' he added, following Jago down the street. There was no missing the diner, which proclaimed its bovine boast in the form of a huge wooden steer perched on the overhanging veranda.

★ ★ ★

The chimes sounding from the church clock had just faded out when the

124

furtive robbers flitted like shadows down the narrow alley that connected Main Street with Kaibab. On the corner at the far end was Cresswell's dry-goods store swathed in darkness. Abutting it was the sturdy brick premises of the Standard Railroad Company, likewise in darkness.

Santee peered up and down the street.

He gave a grunt of approval. Nobody in sight. All the action was along Main, this street being primarily devoted to commercial enterprises.

Flannery led them back into the comforting gloom of the alley.

'Here's the window.' He pointed to the latched half-open entry.

'It'll need a thin wiry dude to crawl through there and open the door,' remarked Padora rather sceptically.

All eyes focused on Laramie Wixx. He was the smallest.

The man from Wyoming sighed.

'OK. Someone help me up,' he said, removing his large Texas sombrero and handing it to Padora.

Following a few terse grunts and accompanied by a measure of squirming contortions, he managed to wriggle through and drop silently down to the floor. Less than a minute later all five were inside the back storeroom of the mercantile.

'Right, boys,' ordered Santee. 'You all know what to look for. Let's get to it. Sooner we're through that goddamned brick wall, the sooner Jago can do his bit.' Leaving Padora, who had been delegated to keep watch, they entered the main body of the store. 'And no lights,' growled the gang leader. 'We don't want any snoopers pokin' around.'

Luckily, it was a clear night. The moon's silvery glow shone through the windows offering sufficent illumination for them to find the necessary items for the heist. Having already surveyed the interior, Chip Flannery was able to direct the others to the appropriate shelves.

They had only been inside the store

for two minutes when a raucous barking from a roaming pack of dogs shattered the nervous silence. Had this four-legged faction sensed their presence?

Everybody froze. With bated breath they anxiously waited. Hands rested on gun butts in readiness. A couple of pistol shots rang out, accompanied by growled imprecations. But the gunfire was not aimed at the intruders. A squeal of pain informed those inside the store that the mystery gunman had found at least one canine target. The brutal response was enough to disperse the pack.

For a further ten minutes, nobody moved a muscle. Only the gentle sough of constricted breathing broke the quietude.

It was Santee who eventually concluded that the unexpected diversion had passed on its way.

'OK, boys,' he rasped through clenched teeth. 'Back to work.'

It was a further fifteen minutes

before they had amassed all the equipment deemed necessary for breaking through the connecting wall and then blowing open the safe. Cautiously, they hauled it upstairs to the second floor.

Everybody was detailed to help break through the double layering of brick. Even Duke Santee, who normally spurned menial labour, was forced to get his hands dirty in order to push the grinding task forward. Coats were discarded as sweat poured off the raiders.

A cloying mixture of brick and cement dust soon filled the air, making it difficult to breathe. Flannery was sent down into the store for some bottles of ginger soda to slake their thirsts.

Once the first layer of brick had been penetrated, Santee decided he needed a breather. Old enough to be the daddy of the bunch, he reckoned he had earned a rest.

'Gonna spell that lazy critter downstairs,' he announced brusquely while trying to shake the clinging detritus from his person. 'Send him back down once you've broken through.'

A caustic glower challenged anybody to argue. Only when he'd disappeared down the stairs did Wixx voice his own view on the major's stamina.

'That guy ain't up to it no more,' he railed. 'Somebody oughta tell him it's time to step down. Let a younger dude take over.'

'That fella being you, I suppose?' shot back Flannery.

'You got a beef with that?' challenged Wixx, squaring his stocky shoulders.

Flannery shrugged a disclaimer. 'Then you'd best be telling him,' he countered. Even though the Wyoming gunslinger was faster on the draw, the younger man stood his ground unfazed.

'And I will once this caper's over, don't think I won't,' huffed Wixx, hammering at the wall in a attempt to emphasize his tough persona.

Dawn was approaching before they eventually broke through the thick skin of the building. A further hour had passed before a hole was fashioned big enough for a man to squirm through.

And that man was Lee Jago.

Scuttling across to the large floor safe, he carefully examined it from all angles to determine how best to set the charge. Three pairs of covetous peepers followed his every move.

'Any problems?' asked Santee, anxious to get on with the job.

Lee ignored the query as he calculated the settings. No way was he going to be rushed into making a mistake. Just like a feisty dame, dynamite was a tricky substance that demanded the utmost care and attention. Failure to accord it sufficient respect and the stuff would kick you in the teeth.

Too much and the contents of the safe would be incinerated, too little would merely dent the sturdy brute. After what seemed like an eternity, he had it all worked out. He proceeded to set the charge.

'Bring the mattresses through and lay

them over the safe,' he said curtly.

Santee and Flannery manhandled the cumbersome items through the hole and positioned them as directed by the dynamite expert.

'Now fasten them to the safe with these ropes.' Lee was enjoying his new-found sense of power over these hardened killers. 'Easy there,' he snapped at Santee. 'Mind you don't disturb the charges. Don't want these little devils going off too soon, do we?'

The gang leader grimaced, but held himself in check. They needed this critter — for now!

One final check by the engineer ensured that nothing had been over-looked.

Outside, an owl emitted a mournful hoot. It was answered by the pitiful howling of the injured cur.

Reeling out the fuse wire, Jago backed towards the hole, passing the reel and all-important detonator to Santee. Then he scrambled back through, screwed the connecting wires on to the detonator body and hauled up the plunger.

'OK! This is it, boys,' he announced with a cheeky grin, eyeballing them each in turn. 'Ready?'

Nobody replied. They were too nervous.

Fixing the gang boss with a wry smirk, Lee pressed down on the plunger.

For the briefest of moments, nothing happened. A knife could have sliced through the tense atmosphere.

Then a muffled roar assaulted their ears. The wall trembled, appearing to bulge inwards. White smoke intermingled with feathers from the shredded mattresses forced a passage through the ragged hole.

Lee waited until the flying debris in the other room had settled before venturing to look through the hole.

'Has it worked?' asked an edgy Duke Santee recalling his last venture in the use of high explosives.

'Take a look for yourself,' replied Lee.

Santee held his breath while tentatively peering through the gap. Tendrils of smoke hung around what looked like a war zone. The room was totally devastated. But there in the centre stood the safe, rock solid, but with its six-inch steel door hanging loose.

A gurgled croak emerged from the gang leader's gaping mouth. Weathered skin drawn tight as a whore's ass, he crawled through the narrow gap.

But what about the greenbacks? Was the dough still useable?

Hesitantly, he approached the safe, hardly daring to look. His face registered pure fear as he reached inside. It felt like sticking your mitt into a rattler's nest. The others looked on, wide-eyed and agog, speechless with tense anticipation, Lee Jago no less edgy than the others.

The hand emerged clutching a thick bundle of notes: used ten-dollar bills, and not a single one was charred. Quickly he removed some more. All were intact. Not a mark on them.

'We've done it, boys.' The whispered comment emerged as a choking grunt.

'Yee-haar!' hollered a more voluble Chip Flannery, running his hands over a bundle of notes. 'We're rich! I ain't seen this much dough in my whole life.' His eyes bulged in awestruck delight.

Even Jago was ecstatic that his plan had worked.

'Now all we gotta do is get outa here in one piece.' As usual it was Wixx who brought them crashing back down to earth.

'Laramie's right,' agreed Santee. 'Get this dough bagged up so's we can make a quick getaway.'

Once all the money had been packed into saddle-bags, Santee ordered Lee to stay behind as rearguard.

'We can't move fast, due to the weight of this dough,' he replied to Lee's suspicious frown. 'Someone's gotta watch our backs.'

'And what'll I use to deter any pursuit?' demanded the dynamite man vehemently. 'Bare fists ain't going to be much use against hot lead.'

'They have a full rack of guns down in the store,' responded Santee. 'And Laramie here will stay and keep you company. Make sure you don't come to no harm.' The sardonic jibe was not lost on Jago. But he purposely chose to ignore it.

Meaningful glances passed between the two outlaws.

Wixx nodded. He knew what had to be done.

# 9

## Flies in the Ointment

The sun had barely made it over the Mogollon Plateau when Duke Santee led his men along Kaibab Street. Once the gang had crossed the railroad track a hundred yards beyond the Flagstaff Halt, he led them along a minor trail up on to the Coconino Divide. His intention was to make a wide circular detour before heading south back to the hideout at Buffalo Wash.

Lee Jago peered through the office window.

After watching the group of riders disappear from view behind the ungainly bulk of the railroad water tower, he scanned both ends of the street below. A lone burro could be seen pursuing an erratic course down the middle of the thoroughfare as the stiffening breeze stirred up the dust. Nothing else moved.

Sunday morning was never a time for early risers. Rebel-rousers were sleeping it off, while the respectable elements of the town were enjoying a welcome respite from their labours. Nobody, it appeared, had cottoned on to the fact that their railroad company had been robbed.

Lee smiled as he pitched a look of disdain towards the damaged portrait of the current president of the Standard Pacific hanging crookedly on the charred wall of the office. The poor sap was in for a shock when news of this caper reached his ears.

The glance, however, revealed more than just the president's bloated gaze. Outlined on the floor beneath the picture, a sharply etched silhouette could be seen moving towards him from behind. Its clearly defined configuration brought a lump to his throat.

The sun-cast shadow of a raised arm clutching a lethal Bowie knife brought home to Lee the stark reality of his precarious situation.

So that was why Santee had left him behind in the capable hands of Laramie Wixx. Capable of cold-blooded murder, was all. The blood-lusting gunman had obviously been given prior orders to get rid of the gang's excess baggage now that he had served his purpose. And a dose of cold steel would keep the lid on their iniquitous scheme.

Well, two could play at that game.

Lee's father had trained him from an early age in the Chinese martial art of Kung Fu. Now was the moment to put those skills into practice.

Sensing his ambusher to be no more than a yard behind him, Lee made a fluid swing to the left just as the deadly blade lunged. It sliced through the air, but encountered no resistance. The exposed back of the proposed victim had suddenly shifted. Pivoting on his right leg, arms akimbo and mouthing a guttural attacking chant Lee jabbed an outstretched left foot towards the groin of his startled opponent.

Shock registered on the gaping visage of the diminutive outlaw. But he quickly recovered, swivelling his hip to shield sensitive areas from the potentially lethal blow. Luckily for him, it merely grazed his leg.

'So this is how it's meant to end,' rasped Lee, settling into the classic Kung Fu stance. 'I should have figured on such treachery from a bunch of thieving skunks.'

A mirthless leer from Wixx needed no interpretation.

The two antagonists warily circled one another. Wixx was anxious to finish the job. He had not anticipated any resistance. And the longer this débâcle was prolonged, the more chance there was of the robbery being discovered. A worried frown pushed aside the arrogant assurance of seconds before.

He lunged with the knife, a straight jab to the face. But Lee was not to be caught that easily. He swayed back on his heels out of reach. Now it was his turn to smile. The sneering grimace only served to incense the outlaw. The engineer's self-assured mien was a deliberate ploy to goad tactical errors from his opponent.

It worked.

A bestial growl erupted from between bared teeth.

'Damn yer blasted hide,' Wixx railed angrily. 'I'll cut out yer liver and feed it to that howlin' mongrel.'

Not only was the injured creature showing no signs of imminent demise, its caterwauling appeared to be increasing in volume. Pretty soon, it would attract unwelcome human intervention. Both men realized this. The stakes for a quick end to the deadly contest had suddenly been upped.

Slashing and jabbing, Wixx pressed forward the attack. Lee backed off. His focused vision never left his opponent. Dodging and weaving to avoid the Bowie's razored edge, he waited for the moment when he could deliver the killing blow.

But so intent was he on avoiding the lethal blade that he tripped over some debris and went sprawling on to his back.

Wixx immediately saw his opportunity. Reversing the knife in his hand, he made to throw it at his helpless opponent. Quick as a flash, Lee scooped up a handful of rubble and threw it into his antagonist's face. Wixx cried out, knuckling the dust from his eyes. At the same time he backed off, allowing Lee to scramble back to his feet.

Grabbing hold of a broken chair the half-breed flung it at the outlaw. In the nick of time, Wixx was able to parry it away with his arm. Once again the pair of gladiators circled one another, each attempting to gain an advantage.

Lee decided it was time to try subterfuge. Relaxing his lean frame, he pretended to be tired, allowing his arms to drop.

Wixx saw his opportunity and dived in for the kill, delivering a vicious slice that would have effectively terminated the deadly contest forthwith had it connected. The ruse enabled the martial artist to duck and step to one side. The blade hissed by overhead, causing Wixx to over-balance.

He stumbled forward, at which point Lee brought the rigid side of his hand down on to the critter's exposed neck. A brittle snap was enough to inform him that the guy was done for.

Wixx slumped to the floor without uttering another sound.

The savage end to the contest brought home to Lee how utterly exhausted he was mentally. The encounter had also taken a more physical toll. He was bleeding from a slash that had opened up his left arm. Lee's brain felt like mush as he sucked in air while resting on his haunches.

But he knew that there was little time to waste. He had to get away.

After tying his bandanna around the wound, Lee unbuckled the outlaw's gunbelt and slung it around his own waist. At least he now had a weapon. Kung Fu was ideal for close-quarter combat, but a firearm was essential over distance.

Lee slipped down the back stairs and gingerly opened the door leading on to the alley beside Kaibab Street. He stepped out, and made for his tethered horse.

But the noise occasioned by the robbery had not gone unnoticed.

'Hold on there, mister,' came a gruff voice from behind. 'What the hell are you doin' in the company office at this early hour?'

Lee stumbled to a halt. The sudden challenge had taken him by surprise. But he instantly recognized the voice as belonging to his arch enemy: the detestable Rafe Boondock. Lee's back stiffened as the Irishman continued: 'And what was that explosion I heard? You got some explainin' to do, fella. Now turn around slowly and drop that hogleg.'

Boondock must have come across from the station. And the rat had got the drop on him. Lee was no gunslinger. But he knew that complying with the varmint's demand would leave him wide open to being gunned down while resisting arrest. The scurvy railroader would never take the chance of letting him escape a second time.

A tight-lipped smile split his dusky visage.

Swivelling on his heel he slapped leather, thumbed back the hammer on the short-barelled Colt and snapped off a couple of shots. Both were wide of the mark, but the dispatch of hot lead in his direction was enough to confuse the railroad man.

But only for an instant. Stepping back a couple of paces, Boondock brought his own pistol to bear.

Panic and the fear of being hit in the lethal exchange was felt by both men, causing their gunplay to go awry. Bullets slammed into the walls, chewing lumps of wood out of doorframes. Smoke blurred their outlines making it difficult to see properly. One slug lifted Lee's hat from his head, another plucked at his sleeve, sending a jolt of fire down his already injured arm.

The engineer emitted a startled howl of pain and a vitriolic oath vented in his tongue of origin. That was when Boondock recognized his opponent.

'You!' he snarled. 'So that's why the prison wagon was ambushed. Them skunks wanted a dynamite man to help them rob the company safe.'

There was no point trying to persuade the Irishman that he had been forced into carrying out the safe job. Boondock would not believe him. Nor would he want to.

Backing towards his mount, Lee fired one last time, but the hammer clicked on an empty chamber. Cussing in desperation he flung the useless hunk of metal at the advancing form of the burly foreman. It struck the Irishman on the temple, temporarily neutralizing any form of retaliation. The lull was enough for Lee to scramble into the saddle and spur off down the empty street.

Although he doubted it would be empty for very long. The rattle of gunfire was bound to have attracted the attention of the resident lawdog. And Lee wanted to be well out of reach before he arrived on the scene.

The lucky strike had only been a glancing blow, enabling Boondock to recover his wits quickly. Shaking the fuzziness from his head, he snapped off a last shot at the back of the disappearing engineer before entering the railroad headquarters. He hurried up the stairs and entered the main office. The scene of total devastation punched him in the guts with the force of a stampeding herd of mavericks.

Mouth hanging low, he stared around the dynamite-blasted room. The safe door hung askew. A quick glance revealed that it had been completely cleared. Not a single dollar bill remained.

Mouthing a lurid curse, Boondock turned to go when a low groan stayed his feet. It came from behind a

146

splintered desk. Hurrying round, he saw a little guy painfully struggling to raise himself. Ever since he had happened upon this outlandish situation, the Irishman's cunning brain had been working overtime. There had to be some means of turning the robbery to his advantage.

And here it was.

The outlaw's neck was bent at an unnatural angle. It was clearly broken. In truth the varmint should be dead. Boondock cradled the badly injured man in his arms.

'Get me to a doctor,' croaked the distressed outlaw.

'Sure thing, fella,' assented Boondock. 'Just as soon as you tell me where your buddies are holed up.'

'Go piss in a bucket!' Wixx spat, blood dribbling from his twisted mouth.

'Suit yerself, mister,' said Boondock, clumsily tossing the dying outlaw aside and getting to his feet.

Wixx howled in pain.

'A-all right,' he stammered. 'I'll tell

yuh. But promise me you'll bring a doc straight away.'

'Would I lie to you?' sneered the crafty fox grinning from ear to ear.

If he wanted to receive medical attention Laramie Wixx had no choice but to trust the smirking Irishman.

'And you'll speak up fer me?' gabbled Wixx, 'Tell the sheriff I helped get the dough back?'

Boondock responded with an icy grin.

'OK,' muttered the dying outlaw. He breathed deep before continuing. 'Here's how it is. We have a cabin hidden away on the banks of Buffalo Wash. That's where the boys have taken the loot. We intended divvying up once I got back. Now get me that sawbones. You promised.'

'Aaaah, me young fella,' tutted Boondock, tongue clicking as he mockingly shook his head. 'Now aren't I the biggest lyin' bastard yuh ever did see.' He picked up the deadly blade dropped by Wixx and tested the edge. 'The sawbones regrets that he can't make it. Say howdy to Mr Bowie.'

Like a hungry sidewinder sizing up its next meal, glittering eyes held the stricken outlaw in a deadly embrace. The evil grin widened as the blade was driven up into the helpless guy's shivering torso.

Wixx gasped, his body arched as vital organs convulsed, their life force fast ebbing away. Blood spewed from his open mouth.

No time was wasted by the killer in fruitless consideration of the consequences that cold-blooded murder would inevitably unleash. A swift departure from the town was essential before that nosy sheriff happened along. Although he knew that Mort Lanning would have spent the night with Miss Maybelle. The soiled dove ran the Cat's Whiskers bordello on Winslow Street. No way would the randy lawdog be over-eager to rouse himself at this early hour on a Sunday morning.

Boondock had it all worked out.

He would make himself indipensable to the Rough Riders by leading them to the place where Lee Jago resided. The engineer would now be hotfooting it back up north to be with that tasty wife of his at Moccasin Flats on the edge of the Painted Desert. Such an offer was bound to be worth a substantial cut of the proceeds.

Santee would surely want to have his revenge on the skunk who had killed one of his gun hands. Not to mention ridding himself of the only other guy who knew the whereabouts of the gang's secret hideout. Boondock couldn't resist an acerbic chuckle at his cunningly audacious scheme.

It was instantly replaced by a mordant scowl.

The owners of the Standard Pacific would bitterly regret not conferring upon Rafe Boondock the reward he reckoned was due following his single-handed capture of the skunk who had tried to kill Brad Straker. For a railman with his experience, promotion up to management level should have been automatic.

Yet not even a substantial bonus had been forthcoming. All he had been offered was a miserly job in charge of security at the Flagstaff depot. It was an insult. Worst of all, there were no more Iucrative sidelines to swell his meagre paypacket.

Another disgruntled gripe rumbled deep within Boondock's barrel chest. Duke Santee ought to welcome a guy of his stature, especially now the gang numbers had been so depleted.

# 10

## Wrong Place, Wrong Time

'That darned squirt oughta been back afore now,' grumbled Santee, imbibing another slug of Charlie Padora's potent brew. 'How long does it take to remove one greenhorn engineer?'

None of the others deemed it prudent to voice an opinion. Best to let the simmering gang boss alone, especially once he started on the hooch. Padora quietly disappeared outside to chop some more logs for the fire, seeing as how it was his turn for chow rota. The old jigger frowned. It seemed like these days he did more cooking than any of the others.

Flannery retired to a far corner of the room to read the dime novel he had lifted from the store in Flagstaff. The garishly imaginative stories had found a ready market among those who had little notion of the true nature of the Western frontier. Their appearance on the shelves of general stores in recent years had prompted numerous gullible boobies to seek out the supposedly glamorous lifestyle on offer.

Flannery chuckled to himself. Such turkeys soon had their eyes opened. The young outlaw had enjoyed baiting the newcomers who quickly learned that popular literature and real life were as far removed as a snowstorm in the desert. Nonetheless, he found the charismatic allure that they depicted fascinating. Indeed, Chip liked to imagine himself in the position of the hero, especially when he was a sharp-shooting tough guy who always won over the prettiest gal in town.

It was late afternoon when a steady drumming of hoofbeats cut through their lethargic torpor. Shrugging off the mind-numbing effects of the moon-shine Santee grabbed his rifle and stumbled over to the small front window of the cabin.

A quick glance was enough to indicate that the approaching rider was a stranger. This dude's sudden appearance did not bode well. All the indications pointed to Wixx having failed in his cut-throat task. That supposition was backed up by Padora.

'Ain't that Laramie's sorrel?' questioned the old guy.

Santee emitted an angry snarl.

Levering a shell into the breech, he called for the rider to draw rein. Steam rose from heaving flanks as the snorting cayuse stumbled to a halt. It had clearly been ridden hard.

'Slide outa that saddle real slow, mister,' Santee snapped, gesturing with the rifle that non-compliance would result in terminal lead poisoning, 'and keep yer hands where I can see 'em.'

Gingerly forsaking the protection afforded by the cabin, the three outlaws emerged from cover. Their guns warily panned the bleak terrain in case this was some trap set up by an enterprising lawdog.

But the guy was alone.

'What d'yuh want, fella?' demanded Santee. His finger tightened on the trigger. 'And how come you're ridin' that cayuse?'

Boondock blanched, fully aware of the very present threat. But he quickly recovered his composure.

Sucking in a deep breath he launched into his prepared dialogue. Truth and fabrication were easily reconciled in Rafe Boondock's disingenuous mind. But the spiel he had worked out in his head during the protracted ride to Buffalo Wash tripped effortlessly off the silvery Irish tongue.

He spoke of his discontent with the railroad hierarchy, asserting that the gang needed to swell their numbers. He also acquainted them with his knowledge of railroad organization, not to mention the invaluable assistance he could provide in avenging the death of Laramie Wixx. It was a well-prepared and convincing exposition.

But the last proposal did not accord

well with Santee, who regarded the gunman's failure as beneath contempt. He was also aware of the Wyoming tough's leadership ambitions. Perhaps it was no bad thing that Wixx was out of the picture. Now he could re-establish his authority.

And it was certainly true that another man was gonna be needed in the future. They'd gotten a heap of dough from that safe. But split three ways — four if he took this guy on — it wouldn't last more than a couple of months.

'That useless critter couldn't nobble a flea in a jamjar,' the gang boss scoffed. 'Gettin' rid of Jago should have been a piece of cake. Now the dude's gone and disappeared.'

The newcomer shook his head.

'I figure different,' he replied, eager to please. 'Let me help you guys complete the task.'

'How can you help?' asked Flannery.

'I know where the skunk hangs out,' stressed Boondock. 'And he was leaking like a sieve when he kicked out of Flagstaff. So you guys can bet your bottom dollar that's where he'll be heading. That Chinky wife of his will provide all the nursing and homely comforts he needs.'

Having listened quietly to the Irishman's suggestions Charlie Padora stepped forward, thumbs hooked into his gunbelt. Removing his battered hat, the old guy scratched his thinning pate.

'Got me a problem here, mister,' wheezed the old moonshiner, gathering his thoughts.

'And what might that be?' replied Boondock confidently.

'How come you was able to find this hideout?'

It was a question that had not occurred to the others. Grim faces fastened on to the cocky redhead, awaiting an answer.

Boondock responded with barely a flicker.

'Your man was able to give me directions afore he pegged out.' A convincing tone of regret punctuated the reply. 'I tried to help him, but it was no good. That murderin' yeller-belly had skewered him good. He died in my arms, poor fella.'

The interview appeared to have gone in Boondock's favour as the gang leader slowly nodded.

'OK, mister,' he said following a brief deliberation with his confederates. 'You're in.'

★ ★ ★

Chuan Li was sweeping the front veranda of the house when she first noticed the swirling cloud of dust on the sagebrush plain to the south.

The building had yet to be completed. Piles of sawn timber lay alongside in readiness for adding the second storey. Perched on a raised terrace above the flood basin of the Little Colorado, the land known as Moccasin Flats had been a wedding present from her husband's family.

Never a day passed without Chuan

anxiously pining for the missing rail-road engineer. And the girl was only too mindful of his disappearance following the ambush of the prison wagon at the Devil's Switchblade. Officers of the law had been quick to ascertain whether he had returned to the family home. They had exhorted her to inform the sheriff's office in Flagstaff should the fugitive put in an appearance.

But since then, nothing. Not knowing whether he was dead or alive was the worst part. Some day, Chuan knew he would return. And she was willing to wait, however long it took. Until then, all she could do was hope and pray.

Shielding her eyes against the glare from the overhead sun, the Chinese girl tried to focus on the unusual phenomenon. It was moving slowly and heading her way. Few visitors ever arrived from that direction.

Gradually the hazy outline of a lone rider emerged from the shimmering mirage.

It was another ten minutes before the

dust-caked horse plodded into the yard. The heads of both animal and rider were bowed with exhaustion. It was clear that the man had been wounded. His shirt was a mess of dried blood. As his mount stumbled to a halt, the figure swayed alarmingly in the saddle.

Chuan gasped as she recognized her husband.

'Jianguo! Jianguo!' she cried, rushing over to help him down. 'What has happened to you, my husband?' In times of stress, the girl always reverted to his Chinese name.

But Lee Jago was knocking on the door of the grim reaper. He had lost a lot of blood. Sliding out of the saddle, he tumbled in a heap on to the hard ground.

He was a big man compared to his wife's diminutive stature. But desperation imbues the most delicate of creatures with untold strength. After dabbing his lips with cooling drips of water, she dragged him into the house and lifted him effortlessly on to the large brass bedstead.

No time was lost in seeking explanations. Those would come later. More vital was the need to remove the bullet from his shoulder, and prevent any infection. Luckily for the wounded man, he remained unconscious whilst his wife dealt with the injuries.

It was some hours later when Lee eventually opened his eyes. The darkness of sleep had been replaced by that of night. A half-moon shone through the window, revealing a sight he had never thought to revere again.

In the silvery light, the radiance of his wife's face seemed to be tempered with an equal measure of anxiety. Lovingly, he held her hand. His mouth opened ready to speak. But Chuan placed a finger over his lips. Her mesmeric smile brought a flush to his pallid cheeks.

'Sshh now, my dearest. Talk later.' The words washed over Lee like melted butter. The lilting cadence was like a breath of fresh air. 'First get strength back. Bullet jammed into shoulder blades was difficult to extract. But Chuan Li not give up. Find sneaky hunk and grab him.' She raised a tin bowl and rattled the offending item.

They both laughed, but the effort brought a wince of pain from the patient. 'You rest now,' soothed Chuan. 'Make good recovery.'

Lee forced himself up on to one elbow. He knew that his wife's caution was well meant. But time was not on their side.

'We can't stay here,' Lee murmured, shaking his head. 'Not safe. Gang will come after me. Gotta leave.' The words emerged in a staccato burst due to his injuries. 'Go stay with my uncle Huojin Soo. It'll give us space to figure out what to do next.'

'But you not well enough to move,' protested Chuan. The fearful apprehension clouding her satin features was emphasized in the flickering candle flame. Tears dribbled down her pale cheeks as she added, 'Not want lose husband again.'

But Lee was adamant.

Already he was thinking about how best to fix these turkeys once and for all. A scheme was needed to lure Santee into a trap and retrieve the stolen loot. He hoped it would gain him some credence with the state governor, who was sympathetic to the difficulties faced by ethnic minorities such as the Chinese.

'Fix up the flatbed with a mattress and blankets,' he urged. 'That should help ease the journey. It ain't that far to Cedar Ridge.' His eyebrows met in a grim frown. 'Stay here another day, honey, and we're both done for.'

★　★　★

Barely more than an hour after Chuan Li had whipped up the horses and left Moccasin Flats with Lee comfortably ensconced in the rear of the wagon, two weary riders drew up outside the house. They had arrived from the opposite direction, which explained why they had not encountered the fugitives.

Big Jim Corrigan and his partner Squint Fowler were heading south-east. Itinerant cowpokes, they hoped to link up with one of the numerous cattle outfits operating across the border in New Mexico. A jasper by the name of Billy Bonney, better known as the Kid, had told them that the Tunstall Ranch in Lincoln County needed extra hands for the autumn round-up.

'Anybody home,' hollered Fowler as they drew up outside the deserted homestead. 'Just a couple of wandering rannies after a night's hospitality.'

It was the generally accepted custom among Western homesteaders to welcome strangers and provide them with vittles and a bed for the night, if only in the hayloft. As such, drifters like Fowler and Corrigan could easily travel across country without any hardship while looking for work. The system worked well. And if a house proved to be unoccupied, then it was common practice to make use of the facilities, leaving a note upon departure.

Corrigan leaned forward over the roan's head, his eyes peeled for any signs of activity. Nothing. Not even a hen on the scratch. But there was no shortage of evidence indicating recent occupation: a prominent woodpile, tools lying around, a curtain flapping from an open window. All the same, the place had the appearance of being deserted.

'Looks like the place has been abandoned,' observed the big cowboy fingering his black moustache uncertainly. 'Kinda strange, ain't it?'

'More to the point,' commented Fowler rolling his good eye, 'We're gonna have to fix our own supper.'

Corrigan couldn't help but laugh.

'Can't you never stop thinkin' about yer stomach?' he quipped, nudging his horse up to the front of the homestead. 'OK, boy, let's be makin' ourselves at home.'

'And it's your turn for rustlin' up some chow,' said Fowler. Then, with a derisive dig, he added, 'Just so long as it ain't refried beans . . . again.'

Darkness had settled over the house and the two cowboys were thoroughly enjoying the unexpected bounty that had come their way.

'What d'yuh reckon happened here?' asked Big Jim.

His cock-eyed partner responded with a shrug of indifference.

'Who cares,' he said, topping up his coffee mug with a generous measure of homemade liquor. 'This stuff sure packs a wallop, and there's another two jugs in the corner.'

It wasn't long after that the pair of inebriates were flat out in the back room, snoring and dead to the world.

★ ★ ★

'That's the place.'

Boondock pointed to the bold outline of a half-constructed building. Moonlight had stitched a pattern of bright beams across the front yard. Not wishing to announce their presence to the occupants, the four men drew to a halt, intangible shadows lurking in the Stygian gloom.

'Looks deserted to me,' observed Flannery. Indeed, there were no lights on show and no discernible sound emanated from the lone structure.

'They're in there,' insisted Boondock who was keen to assert his part in steering the gang along the right trail. 'With Jago wounded, it's no surprise that they've hit the sack early.'

'We'll give them another half-hour,' said Santee, stepping down from his horse. 'Just to make certain they are asleep. Then we'll torch the place.'

His next remark was aimed at Charlie Padora.

'You got them bottles of coal oil ready?'

'Sure thing, boss,' replied the old jigger, tapping his left saddle-bag. 'Four of them should be more than enough to douse the place and send it up like a Thanksgiving bonfire.' A malevolent chuckle sent an uneasy ripple of trepidation down Rafe Boondock's spine. He hoped he had not bitten off more than he could chew in teaming up with this hard-faced bunch.

The half-hour passed slowly, especially as Santee had banned smoking.

'No sense in givin' our presence away.'

Eventually the order was given. Each man took a side of the building and splashed the inflammable liquid against the wooden walls. The signal to ignite the lethal coal oil was given by Chip Flannery, who had the uncanny ability to mimic the eerie call of a desert owl.

Two short hoots followed by a long one, and four vestas were struck.

In the blink of an eye the house was ablaze.

Tongues of flame licked up the sides of the tinder-dry walls. Emboldened by a mounting breeze the appetite of the conflagration was insatiable. Wooden beams crackled and popped as the flames quickly took hold. In no time, the fire had completely engulfed the entire homestead. Black smoke swirled and twisted around the orange core as if in pain before disappearing into the cheerless backdrop of night.

Nobody could survive such a rampant inferno.

But just in case, Santee had ordered his men to stand back, guns at the ready to shoot down anybody who emerged.

When it became apparent that no living soul had survived the conflagration, Santee called for his men to back off.

'We'll wait until daybreak,' he said. 'By then the fire ought to have burned itself out. If not, we can douse it with water.'

'Why wait?' argued Boondock. 'Anyone in there will have been fried to a crisp.'

Duke Santee stiffened. Moonlight reflected the vicious scowl distorting the gang leader's countenance. A hand shot out and grabbed the bumptious toad by the throat.

'You listen to me, dogbreath,' he

hissed. 'I'm ramroddin' this outfit. And what I say goes. And I say we check out this berg to make certain there are two bodies in there. You got me, fella?' He shook the big Irishman like a dog savaging a bone, jabbing his hog leg up the twitching snout. 'And if'n there ain't, my friend here will be servin' up a lead sandwich.'

'The major ain't kept us outa jail and in the dough all this time by cuttin' corners,' snapped Chip Flannery, in support of his leader. 'You wanna run with us, you toe the line and do as he says.'

'S-sure th-thing, boss,' stuttered the sweating railroader. 'Anything you say. I weren't thinkin' straight.'

Santee pushed the mortified Irish-man aside and lit a cigar, smiling as if nothing untoward had occurred. The casual act made his browbeating of the gang's newest recruit all the more chilling.

'Let's get some shut-eye, boys,' he breezed. 'Once we've made certain that

that slippery galoot and his moll have hit the high trail, there's some serious spendin' of that lovely loot to be gotten through, don't yuh think?'

With a series of light-hearted guffaws the men started arranging their bed-rolls. Rafe Boondock had learned a valuable lesson that he would forget at his peril.

Sun-up found Shotgun Charlie preparing breakfast. Balanced precariously on a flat rock to one side of the fire sat a large blackened coffee pot, its contents bubbling merrily.

Displaying the infinite care learned from salutary experience, the old guy nudged Santee's boot beneath the grubby horse blanket. He waited for the usual griping epithets to dissipate before handing over his morning cup of coffee. Scenting the aroma of frying bacon, Santee was soon fully awake.

The house fire had burnt itself out during the night. Wisps of smoke drifted from the blackened hulk of what remained, which was precious little.

Following a hurried repast Santee ordered his men to search the premises.

'You take the rear,' he said to Boondock. 'Me and Chip will search the main room, while Charlie here gives the outbuildings the once over.' He accorded the assembled outlaws a granite-hard glare as they prepared to go about the grisly task. 'And remember,' he stressed, 'we need to find two bodies. Any more than that is bad luck for them.'

It was the new recruit who made the gruesome discovery in what had once been the bedroom. Boondock's ruddy face paled with shocked horror as the grim reality of what he had brought about struck home.

Was that his conscience lumbering to the fore? Momentarily. But it was soon consigned to an appropriate trash can.

Following their heavy drinking session, Big Jim and his partner had made themselves comfortable in the large double bed. Boondock retched at the sight of the charred corpses, his breakfast spewing out across the blackened husks that had so recently been living human beings.

Now they were barely recognizable as such. The intensity of the conflagration had ensured that identification was impossible. Two bodies sleeping in the marital bed could be no other than those of Lee Jago and his wife.

Affording himself time to gather his wits and compose himself, Rafe Boondock scooped up some of the charred remnants to disguise his weakness. The tough-guy image had to be maintained.

'In here, boss,' he shouted infecting a generous degree of gruffness into the harsh summons. 'You'll sure wanna see this.'

The others quickly gathered in the back room.

'Ain't this enough proof that I been straight with yuh?' Boondock demanded forcefully.

'Sure looks like it, Rafe,' agreed Santee, swallowing hard to prevent his own meal joining that of the Irishman. 'You done well.' He slapped the railroader on the back in praise. 'And for that, you've earned an equal share of the split once we get back to the Wash.'

They were all eager to get back outside to breathe some fresh wholesome air.

'No sense hangin' round now the job's been done,' Santee said as he swung up into the saddle. Fiercely digging his spurs into the big bay stallion, he galloped off. 'We got us some celebratin' that's overdue.'

'Yee-haar!' hollered Flannery as the rest of the gang followed suit. 'I'll sure drink to that.'

# 11

## Partners to the End

It was two weeks before Lee felt well enough to return to their home on Moccasin Flats. Nobody had come after them during his convalescence at the home of Huojin Soo. Clearly both the railroad company and the Santee Gang were unaware of his relationship to the old loco driver. Safe for the time being he knew, however, that life could never be the same again.

Old Huojin had imparted the disturbing news that Governor Jackson had been defeated in the recent elections. His successor was a dyed-in-the-wool redneck who was a stickler for law and order.

A fresh start in another part of the country would have to be arranged. Heading north to Canada seemed the safest option.

The flatbed, along with the buggy he had left in the barn, ought to be enough to transport their possessions back to Cedar Ridge. Then they would make a brief halt to say their goodbyes before leaving for pastures new. As a railroad engineer, Lee knew that with his experience there would be no difficulty in obtaining work. Getting even with Santee and his bunch would have to wait a while.

Such a train of thought was occupying his mind as he crested the low rise that led down to the homestead on the banks of the Little Colorado. What he found there chilled the blood in his veins.

Utter devastation greeted his bulging eyes. Charred beams, black and staring, pierced the azure sky, a brutal indication of the dangerous situation in which both he and his wife were now embroiled. Nothing was left, only burnt remnants. Their life, which should have been idyllic, now promised nothing short of a cursed nightmare.

And it was all his fault.

'Who do this?' cried Chuan Li.

The answer was obvious.

Rafe Boondock had joined up with the Santee Gang and led them here. A shudder of horror gripped his entrails at the thought of what might have happened had they not vacated the house. And now the gang would be searching for them, knowing their prey had slipped through the net. A dazed Chuan stepped down off the wagon and stumbled over to the gaunt remains of her home. Her eyes were brimming with tears as she sank down on her knees. Unable to venture into the charred ruin, her head bowed in abject sorrow.

In some vague hope that he might find something, Lee wandered aimlessly through the ruins.

Then —

A sharp cry cleaved through the grim silence.

Staggering out of the chaotic turmoil, Lee joined his wife. Holding her trembling frame, he quietly apprised her of his gruesome discovery.

'There's two bodies in there.' His voiced cracked with emotion. 'They're badly scorched and unrecognizable.'

'Who could they be?' asked Chuan.

Lee shrugged. 'More'n likely drifters who called by wanting some grub.'

A brief nod from Chuan. It had happened on numerous occasions before.

'Poor fellows,' she sobbed wiping the tears from her blotched cheeks.

'Bad for them,' agreed Lee, 'But good for us.'

'How you mean?' enquired Chuan, frowning.

'Don't you see? The gang must think that they've finished us off.' A hard glint of fiery resolve had replaced the distraught anguish. 'This means we now got the whip hand.' Lee stood, his eyes narrowing. Silently he vowed to seek out and destroy the animals who had perpetrated this heinous atrocity. How to achieve such an end he had no idea. But the determination was there and his aim would somehow be realized.

Chuan could clearly see that her husband was set on a course that might well end in his being finished off permanently. Stubborn, strong-willed and pig-headed — he was all these things. Nothing would shift his decision once it had been established.

Nonetheless, she tried.

'You no gunfighter, Jianguo,' she urged. 'Be killed by bad men. Canada offers new life. Let us go there, now. Forget this . . . ' Her waving arms impotently embraced the havoc around them.

A flinty coldness, obdurate and severe, met the girl's fervent plea. His mind was made up.

'I cannot allow this to go unavenged.' The sombre resolution was expressed in barely more than a taut whisper.

Chuan shrugged, accepting the inevitable.

'So be it,' she agreed. 'But we do this together.'

'No!' rapped Lee. 'It's too dangerous. I will do it alone.'

'Together!' replied Chuan sharply, her own streak of obstinacy challenging the stolid pledge of her husband. 'Or I go Canada without you.'

Lee knew when to surrender. He smiled. It was the first time in three weeks. His face lit up, briefly illuminated by the noonday sun.

'Partners to the end, no matter what.' Chuan echoed the sentiment.

'Duke Santee and his scumbags, then . . . Canada!'

★ ★ ★

'So how you intend fighting these devils?' enquired Lee's uncle, once he had acquainted the driver with his intentions. They were seated round the deal table in Huojin Soo's small house on the edge of Cedar Ridge. Chopsticks clicked as they finished off the last of the delicious beef chow mein.

Lee had been giving the problem

considerable thought during the two-day trek back up north to the small desert town.

'From the short time I spent with Santee,' he said, sipping his coffee. 'I know that he likes to spend his ill-gotten gains in Ash Fork. Maybe I could mosey on down that way and catch him unawares.' An ugly snarl creased the handsome features. 'Then plug his miserable hide.'

'More like crafty fox cook your goose, my esteemed but artless nephew,' responded the grey-haired old Chinaman, twiddling his silvery plait. 'Ash Fork one bad place. Attract unholy crew of bandits because no law. Last marshal shot after two days. Railroad not stop there any more. Go straight through fast as streaking arrow. You go there, gang recognize esteemed self and . . . ' Huojin imitated a shooting pistol. 'Bang! Bang! Goodbye foolish nephew.'

Lee scowled.

'You got any better suggestions?' he asked grouchily, lighting up a corona.

The old man's eyes twinkled.

'Chinese proverb say *Greedy man easiest to deceive.*' He offered a wry smile to his perplexed visitors.

'I not hear that one,' said Chuan Li, frowning.

'Somebody must spread rumour about dispatch of secret gold shipment to attract greedy robbers.' Lee and his wife sat mesmerized by Huojin's lilting inflections. 'Hook in gang to rob train at selected point. Then set ambush to trap them.'

'Not to mention that slimeball, Rafe Boondock,' added the snarling dynamite expert. The proposal had merit but there was still one essential item missing. 'So who can we get to lay their life on the line to bait the trap?'

At that precise moment there was a knock on the door.

Huojin rose from his seat and went to the door.

A burly guy, clad in rough overalls bearing the Standard Pacific logo entered.

'This my ex-fireman, Crank Tanner.' Huojin introduced his visitor by placing emphasis on the fact that Tanner was no longer employed in his previous capacity. Holding up his left hand, the reason was instantly clear. Only two of his fingers remained.

Tanner acknowledged their shocked response by briefly outlining the story behind the loss.

'Huojin has told me all about your problem,' he began, 'and I want to offer my help. I got me three reasons right here to wanna get even with that bunch of varmints. They have a big reckoning due.' He massaged the mutilated left hand, according it a louring grimace. 'After that botched robbery, all the company could offer me was a night-watchman's job in a line cabin. But at least they had the decency to maintain my old level of pay.' The granite expression softened into a warped grin as he added, 'And my right hand ain't hampered none.'

In the snap of a lion's jaw, a .44

Remington had leapt into his fist.

'As you see, my old buddy one fast gunhand.' Huojin smiled.

Tanner went on to explain that nobody would recognize him in Ash Fork. So he could look out for the unmistakable Confederate major who bossed the outlaw gang known as the Rough Riders.

'I know of a loco that's due for being demolished,' continued Soo. 'It's still operational with a single express car tacked on back and is stuck on an abandoned branch line. That is where hold-up will be arranged.'

'Sounds like a good plan,' agreed Lee after they had thrashed out the details. The four allies clinked glasses as they toasted the success of their odd and extremely dangerous mission.

Everything now depended on Duke Santee taking the bait.

# 12

## Setting the Trap

As expected Duke Santee was propping up the bar of the Galloping Goose saloon in Ash Fork. It was a wide-open berg where anything went. Since the last marshal had been given a lethal dose of lead poisoning, most of the more respectable citizens had left.

Only those able to make a living from the unruly elements that now held sway in town had elected to stay. There was big money to be made from serving the needs of unsavoury types on the run. And those wanting a safe haven to hang out until the hue and cry died down felt safe here.

Saloons, cathouses and theatres: all did a thriving trade.

Crank Tanner had been in town for three days before the gang boss deigned to put in an appearance. He was beginning to think that his supposition had been mistaken. To allay any suspicions, the railman had dropped various hints that he was on the run after robbing a Wells Fargo stagecoach near Tucson.

Discreetly seated at the back of the long narrow room, he had an unrestricted field of view.

It was early afternoon when the batwings swung open and a large guy stepped into the hazy gloom of the interior. Tanner gulped, dropping the cards he had been about to deal for yet another game of solitaire.

Duke Santee was instantly recognizable from his old grey uniform, the battered hat with its Confederate insignia adding to the masquerade. Luckily he was alone.

Stifling a laugh that anybody could still be holding a torch for the discredited uniform after all these years, Tanner nevertheless was well aware that this guy had evaded capture for a coon's age. He had also been responsible for the incineration of two innocent victims, not to mention the gunning down of a brakeman. Chuck Wesley might have been a cantankerous old scrope, but he was a friend, someone to be avenged.

But most of all, Crank was harbouring a bitter hatred for the loss of his three fingers. A loss that had effectively terminated his chance of taking over from Huojin Soo when the old driver retired next year.

Suddenly, the Confederate major didn't look so comical.

Tanner stifled an angry growl. He had to play this cool as a mountain stream.

Slowly lifting his burly frame out of the chair, he shouldered a path through the heaving throng of merrymakers to the long mahogany bar. After ordering another beer, he turned to the slouching major, addressing him in a hard no-nonsense voice.

'Duke Santee?'

The gang leader tensed. Nobody except his own men knew he had come to Ash Fork. Assuming a look of arrogant disdain, he slowly turned to face the speaker, quickly sizing him up.

A large guy in his thirties stared back. Five days of black stubble coated a granite face. A cruel mouth, tight-lipped, couldn't hide the frosty glower emanating from a pair of ice-blue peepers. And judging by the low-slung revolver on his right hip, this critter was no tenderfoot.

Tanner sipped his beer while holding the other man's gaze, waiting.

'Who wants to know?' replied Santee curtly.

'The name's Crank Tanner. I was told that Duke Santee had moved up into the big time.'

The gang boss raised his eyebrows. News of his enhanced reputation was welcome. But the sullen glower quickly returned.

'Who told yuh that?'

'Don't matter none,' said Tanner. He signalled the bartender to refill Santee's glass. The task was done instantly. Duke Santee was a good customer, especially following a successful robbery. 'I got me some information for a guy that's into train jobs. Somep'n that involves a secret gold shipment.'

Santee's eyes lit up. Where gold was concerned, he was like most other outlaws. Avoiding any outward display of curiosity, he angled his lofty gaze towards the large mirror behind the bar. Tanner assumed a similar stance. He knew that Santee would be weighing things up in his devious brain.

'Well?' enquired Tanner eventually. 'You interested?'

'Maybe.'

'So maybe' — a pause followed — 'maybe we could do business?'

Santee swung back to face the newcomer.

'Why would some jasper I ain't never set eyes on afore suddenly appear and ask me to rob a train for him?' Suspicion oozed from every pore of his grizzled visage.

'This is why!'

Tanner held up his left hand.

He was staring into the loathsome black heart of the man who had been responsible for the crippling disfigurement. With the greatest effort, he somehow managed to conceal the abhorrence that threatened to derail the plan. His whole being ached to throw down on this vile character and blow him away.

'It was an accident, but the company sacked me,' he snapped, injecting the comment with suitable venom. 'Didn't give me no compensation even though it weren't my fault.'

Santee frowned. Seemed like he'd ridden down this trail once before. Still, the other guy had not played him false. It had just been that goldarned problem with the dynamite. As long as this dude's plan didn't involve high explosives, it was worth a listen.

He gestured towards the stairs at the rear, then turned to address the bartender.

'I'll be in the back room if anybody

wants me,' he rapped.

'Sure thing, Major,' the barkeep shouted back above the discordant clamour. 'Take all the time you need. Molly ain't wanting use of the bed 'til after nine.'

Santee levered himself off the bar and headed for the stairs.

Crank Tanner followed, a thin smile hidden behind the beard growth. Everything was going according to plan. The fish had sensed the bait and been tempted. All that was needed now was for the outlaw to snap it up.

The upper room was decked out entirely in red. From the velvet window drapes down through bed covers to the carpet. It was clearly a boudoir of distinction. Tanner casually wondered if Duke Santee was a regular customer of the so far unseen Molly.

'So what's this about a train job?' enquired Santee, butting in on Tanner's thoughts once they were alone. His face remained deadpan, the voice nonchalant and relaxed. But there was no denying that he was intrigued by this dude's claim regarding a gold shipment.

Tanner then proceeded to explain the details of what was involved, including the best place to stop the train. Nobody outside the rail company would know that the branch line through the Aquarius Mountains to Buckskin had been abandoned, so they wouldn't be disturbed. He even suggested the exact place that logs should be placed across the track to halt the train.

All that he omitted, ostensibly for reasons of security, was the date of the proposed shipment. Tanner reassured the gang boss that the gold was stacked in strongboxes that would not require the use of dynmaite.

'If you agree to my terms,' the railman proposed, 'I'll leave the date with Jake the bartender downstairs. That way there'll be no chance of any double-dealing.'

'You don't trust me?' Santee raised an eyebrow.

'Of course I do, Duke,' replied Tanner, returning the grin with one that was equally cold and devoid of humour. 'As much as I would a cornered sidewinder.'

Santee responded with a sharp chuckle, appreciating the mutually suspicious tension between them.

'Well I hope this delivery ain't too soon,' continued Santee, 'cos I need to get word to the boys. Have them assemble at the hideout.'

'Don't worry none, it ain't for another two weeks,' shot back Tanner. 'Does that mean we have a deal?' he asked, hardly able to contain his delight.

'Guess so,' agreed Santee pouring out a couple of doubles. 'Let's drink to a successful hold-up.'

They clinked glasses.

'And my cut of the loot,' Tanner responded with an oily smile.

Santee didn't acknowledge the addendum to the toast. He had other ideas on that score, ideas he intended keeping strictly to himself.

'One thing you ain't mentioned though,' he then added, leaning forward in an attempt to menace the fireman.

'Yeh?'

'Where will you be while all this action is goin' on?'

'I'm a fireman . . . or was.' A bleak cloud passed across Crank Tanner's eyes before he continued. 'So I'll be stokin' up that blamed loco. For this one trip, the regular guy will disappear. That way I can get the drop on the driver. Make sure he don't do anythin' stupid. Huojin Soo is like a firecracker when he's riled. It'd be just like the old goat to smash straight through the log barricade you boys will have laid across the track.'

# 13

## The Dawn of Aquarius

On the day the trap was due to be sprung, Crank Tanner was on hand before dawn to fire up the old locomotive. Raising enough steam for such a fractious old lady to perform at her best took a heap of time. The others joined him as dawn was breaking over the Aquarians.

Huojin Soo patted the tough iron plates of the loco's tender.

'How she doing?' he asked, while automatically dragging an oily rag over the wheel connecting rods.

'Fine, Mr Soo,' replied Tanner, checking the pressure gauge. 'The old gal's behaving herself for once.'

'We are depending on you,' whispered the pensive driver, as if he were addressing a living creature. 'This important day for you, my beauty.'

Over the last two weeks, they had worked hard to transform the loco from a seized-up rusting hulk into an operational princess of the rails. It had demanded the utmost secrecy in order to prevent any inquisitive eyes from becoming too curious. This had entailed the down-at-heel external appearance of the engine being maintained, much to the regret of Huojin, who would have preferred having her looking pristine on the big day.

Both members of the crew took a stroll round the hissing old matriarch to make a final check that all was in order. Grease points on her wheel bearings were given a last squirt before Huojin announced that he was satisfied.

'All aboard then,' hollered Lee, hoisting himself up into the express car.

He was followed by Chuan Li who had insisted on being included in the mission. She argued that an extra gun inside the car was vital in getting the drop on a hard-bitten gang for whom killing and robbery was second nature.

'Aren't I the best shot with a rifle?' she protested.

'But that's only been at rabbits for the cooking pot,' Lee countered firmly. 'There's a heap of difference aiming to kill a man, no matter what sort of skunk he is.'

'These men would have killed you without second thought,' she said with unblinking resolve. 'Chuan Li not hesitate when time come.'

There was no persuading her to stay behind. And Lee had to admit that he could sure use the extra firepower.

A couple of toots on the whistle and Loco 2655, affectionately named Diamond Lil by Crank Tanner, girded up her powerful loins. Snorting white steam and breathing fire, she lurched forward. The huge drive wheels spun crazily as the brake lever was disengaged before gripping the rails and trundling slowly forward. Black smoke billowed from the tall stack.

Diamond Lil was on the move.

'Yeeehaaa!' squawked a jubilant Crank Tanner, waving his greasy striped cap in the cool morning air. 'We're off!'

Even though they could be heading into the jaws of death, it was a welcome release of tension to be off the starting blocks at last.

★   ★   ★

Duke Santee and his men were hunkered down behind a cluster of rocks. Immediately opposite their position was the large barricade of logs, rocks and axed juniper trees. Santee was confident that even if the train failed to stop, it would be derailed.

It was sited just round a bend in the track where the line emerged from a rock cutting. Out of sight behind some rocks was the flatbed wagon they had brought along to haul away the gold shipment.

Crank Tanner had displayed astute vision in selecting this particular place for the hold-up. A weakness in the soaring phalanx of the north-south orientation of the Aquarius Mountains had enabled the rail company to hack out the narrow gap known as Zodiac Pass.

Beyond, the terrain appeared at first glance to be as flat as a billard table all the way to the line's terminus at Buckskin. Essentially, however, it comprised a myriad of interconnecting gullies and dry arroyos with barely a hint of vegetation to be seen. The railroad skirted the extensive plateau in a huge looping arc. In consequence, this was the only place where a barricade could be erected without it being spotted too soon by an approaching train.

Flannery pricked up his ears.

'It's here, Major,' he declared.

In the distance, the mournful tone of a whistle heralded the imminent arrival of loco 2655 and a fortune in gold bullion.

'Don't forget, boys,' hissed Santee for the third time in the last hour. 'Soon as that sucker stops, me and Chip call on the train guards to surrender. Like as not they'll refuse. And this is where Charlie and Rafe come in.'

The Irishman interrupted with a sigh of irritation.

'Yeah! I know, boss,' he muttered. 'We catch the turkeys by surprise from on the far side of the car.'

'And I let the varmints have it with old Faithful here.' Padora fondly patted the lethal shotgun, once again snapping down the boxlock to check that the twelve bore was loaded. An evil grimace twisted his pitted features. 'No chance of any backchat when this old boy speaks.'

Boondock gave him a brooding look. The old critter was losing his marbles.

'So what yuh waitin fer?' rasped Santee. 'The bastard'll be here in a minute.'

* * *

Lee's jawline tightened.

The plaintive moan of the loco

whistle informed him that they were about to enter Zodiac Pass. He silently prayed that his stars were in the ascendant. An adoring look passed between man and wife.

Briefly they clasped hands, a momentary kiss, a hug. The moment of no return had arrived.

'Partners to the end . . . no matter what.'

The hushed pledge was interrupted by a scuffling at the front door of the express car. Crank Tanner had arrived. Regretfully, they pulled apart as the fireman shouldered through the door, having crawled across the log-filled tender to join them. He had elected to support them in the express car where he figured Santee's assault would be concentrated.

It was to their advantage that the gang believed Tanner to be on their side which gave Huojin Soo the chance to make his presence felt. The old driver hefted a .41 Colt Lightning in readiness for playing his part.

An ominous duskiness enveloped the boxcar as it entered the confines of the pass. The walls of the narrow rift rose sheer on either side, a roar of concentrated sound drowning out Tanner's mouthed: 'Good luck!'

The sentiment was clear. Lee responded with a brief smile.

Rifles cocked and ready, they waited by the open windows. All glass had been removed as a precaution. In no time light flooded back into the car. Almost immediately, a screeching of tortured metal informed the occupants that the driver had applied the brakes.

Shuddering to a halt, Diamond Lil roared her grating displeasure as the brusque command of Duke Santee split the ether.

'Toss yer weapons out and nobody'll get hurt,' he yelled. 'All we want is the gold. Any turkey what resists will get shot down.'

Lee had been prepared for this order. He paused briefly to give the impression the demand was being accorded due consideration.

'OK!' he shouted back. 'We don't want any trouble. No sense getting shot up over someone else's gold.'

To convince the gang leader that he had the upper hand, Lee threw out a couple of old pistols and a flintlock rifle, all empty of ammunition.

'The trick's worked,' hissed a grinning Crank Tanner. 'The varmints are coming out.'

A bearded face minus the grey hat appeared from behind a large boulder. From the other side, Chip Flannery tentatively followed.

A shot rang out from the direction of the locomotive cab. It whined off the rock inches from Santee's exposed head. The gang boss ducked. But it was Flannery who replied, snapping off three shots in rapid succession. He had the satisfaction of hearing a plaintive cry.

Huojin tumbled from the cab and lay still on the ground.

'Got the bastard,' hollered Flannery,

pumping another two slugs into the inert form.

A growl of angry rage erupted from the express car. The howl of anguish from the injured driver told Lee that his uncle had made his play too soon, and had paid the price. The gang had now been warned; this effectively stymied Lee's plan to catch them out in the open. There was only one way forward now.

'They got Huojin,' rapped Lee. 'Now the fat is really in the fire. Let 'em have it.'

Three guns poked through the glassless windows. Soon hot lead was buzzing all around Santee's head like a swarm of angry bees. Spitting and gouging out chunks of rock, the broadside forced the outlaw to back off quickly and take cover behind the boulder.

'Its a trap!' yelled Santee. 'That skunk of a fireman has gone and double-crossed us.'

Then, as suddenly as it started, the

sharp crackle of gunfire ceased.

A heavy silence followed. But it lasted no more than a few seconds, torn apart by the throaty roar of a shotgun.

Santee smiled. Old Faithful was earning his keep.

* * *

Shotgun Charlie and his partner were already in position on the far side of the train when the rattle of gunfire shattered the stillness. And it was coming from inside the car, where the gold bullion was stored.

He might not be the most agile of jiggers these days, but Padora was still a smart cookie. He quickly read the situation.

And it didn't look promising.

The guards were putting up a fight.

But they hadn't reckoned with this wily old dog. Padora gripped the treasured shotgun, easing back both hammers as he quietly mounted the steps at the front while Boondock approached from the rear. The old outlaw indicated that he would go in first.

Boondock had likewise grasped the state of affairs and responded with a quick nod of understanding.

With infinite caution, the old outlaw turned the handle of the door, praying that the guys inside had not seen fit to lock it. A deep sigh of relief issued from clenched teeth. He was in luck. His good fortune held as the door swung open on well-greased hinges.

Briskly stepping inside the car, Padora knew he ought to blast away, even if it did mean shooting a guy in the back. But he couldn't shake off the old notion of giving the other guy an even break. It was a way of operating he had learned during the war, and it had never left him.

'Drop yer weapons and surrender,' he bawled panning the shotgun to cover the three occupants. 'This old boy's got yuh covered.'

But Tanner was having none of it.

Without thinking, he swivelled and snapped off a quick shot at the looming threat. It singed the left side of Padora's head. The old outlaw grunted, lurching back a pace, then let fly with both barrels.

The lethal blast resounded in the enclosed confines of the car. Twin tongues of death billowed from the deadly weapon.

Tanner stood no chance. His gaping mouth slumped open in shock as he staggered back. Desperately he clutched at the gaping hole where his stomach had been in a futile effort to prevent his guts spewing forth. But there was no way back from such a deadly assault. The lumbering fireman slid down the wall, an ugly smear of crimson in his wake.

Smoke filled the room, blurring the outlines of the protagonists.

That gave Lee the chance to bring his own revolver into play. Padora threw his shotgun aside as both men went for their holstered pistols.

Previous such run-ins, too numerous to recount, might once have indicated that the result was a foregone conclusion. But along with poor eyesight, Padora's gun hand had slowed palpably in recent years. To such an extent that even a greenhorn like Lee Jago was able to outdraw him.

Orange flame leapt from the engineer's Smith & Wesson Schofield. The first shot went wide, but the second punched the ageing outlaw in the belly. A strangled howl of anguish was cut short as the third bullet finished the job.

The express car was like a charnel house, blood-spattered and gory.

Lee's chest felt like it was being crushed, but the raging battle was nowhere near over.

The rear door of the car slammed back on its hinges as Rafe Boondock joined the ructions. His grey matter was stupified into submission on perceiving what he took to be a pair of ghosts. How had these two jerks managed to survive the fire? It didn't seem possible.

Chuan Li had been peppering the rocky enclave behind which Santee and Flannery were crouching. The temporary respite provided by Boondock gave her the opportunity to bring her own rifle to bear on this new attack.

The ratcheting back of the Winchester's lever stung the Irishman's lethargic brain back into motion. He let fly. Hot lead belched forth. And that would have been the end for the Chinese girl had the lethal bullet not struck the raised long gun. The rosewood butt disintegrated, slivers of polished wood flying off at a tangent.

Chuan screamed.

And not just on account of the ghastly fear that was overwhelming her own brain. The force of the blow had saved her life, but in so doing, had flung her backwards. Her head had cracked against the hard wooden wall momentarily stunning her. She sank to the floor.

A crazy growl of delight erupted from

the grinning Irishman.

'Say yer prayers, Chink,' he snarled, jabbing the pistol forward once again. 'You shoulda stayed home, not mixed it with the bad guys.'

But the delay had given Lee the chance to bring his own gun round. He wasted no time uttering idle threats of retribution.

Aim and fire!

Aim and fire!

The first bullet lifted the Irishman's battered derby from his squat head. The second gouged a chunk out of his right ear. He let out a frantic wail of pain, slapping his free hand to the bleeding appendage.

Lee jumped to his feet, intending to finish the duel permanently.

But his gun was empty.

Suddenly the tables had been turned.

Screaming like a banshee, he launched himself at the startled figure in the open doorway.

'Aaaaaaaagh!'

Boondock attempted to bring his gun

up, but he had been caught unawares. Head lowered, Lee punched the breath from the slack torso. Boondock's gun flew out of his hand.

Both men went down.

But it was the stocky Irishman who recovered first. Scrambling to his feet, the redhead grabbed Lee's shirt front and slammed a bunched fist into his face. A howl of grim satisfaction emerged from the scowling maw on seeing the engineer's head snap back, blood oozing from a split lip. It was quickly followed up by a stunning left hook that cracked against Lee's jaw, rattling his teeth.

Another baying whoop indicated that Boondock was thoroughly at home in a fist fight. Brawling was second nature to him.

'This is where I finish you off good and proper, me fine bucko,' he growled, slipping a knife from the sheath attached to his boot. 'This fella did for that turkey Wixx. Now it's your turn to make his acquaintance. Third time lucky, eh? No way are you gonna escape again.'

A manic chuckle, ugly and macabre, accompanied the deft wielding of the deadly weapon. Slivers of sunlight beaming in through the open window glinted off the polished steel blade.

Lee lashed out with his boot. Boondock yelped as the blow connected, giving Lee the chance to shake free of the brute's grasp.

Backing off, he wiped the blood from his mouth while desperately trying to dispel the numbing effects of the brutal assault. Faced by such a seasoned combatant, he was out of his depth, and knew it. He swallowed, but his throat felt dry as the desert wind. Desperately he looked around for a weapon to parry the lethal jabs of the knife.

There was nothing to hand.

But Lady Luck was about to smile on him.

In the thick of the action, Boondock had forgotten about the presence of Chuan Li. Having recovered from the numbing blow to the head, there was no way the Chinese flower was about to lose her husband to this rabid dog. Boondock's gun had landed close by. Quickly she leaned across and took hold of the heavy revolver. Dragging back the hammer, she aimed the gun and fired.

It was the last bullet. It struck the advancing tough in the head. He cried out once, crumpled to the floor, then lay still.

Choking clouds of gunsmoke filled the close confines of the express car. A figure staggered towards her. There was a lump in her throat. Then Lee was beside her. She clung to him, murmuring endearments.

'Thank the gods you are safe,' she sobbed.

But the game was nowhere near finished.

'You keep those critters busy outside . . . ' Lee paused in mid-flow. His heart was pounding like a steam hammer as he desperately tried to steady the thumping in his chest. '. . . while I check that these dudes are both goners.'

Although her head was throbbing, Chuan nodded without any hesitation. This was no time for dithering. Both their lives were at stake. And with only herself and Jianguo remaining, their situation was still extremely precarious.

Her breathing came in short pants as she tried to remain calm.

Lee quickly reloaded the revolver and passed it back. Brushing strands of black hair off her face, Chuan rested the gun on the edge of the window frame and pulled the trigger.

The shots were randomly aimed. They had no hope of striking a target. But their significance was not lost on Duke Santee. He now realized that Padora and the new guy had failed to take out the occupants of the express car. Indeed, they were probably dead.

'Hey, Chip!' he called. 'You still there?'

'Sure thing, boss,' replied the young

tough. 'What we gonna do?'

Santee had been mulling over his options. There was only one course of action open if he was to pull this off and escape in one piece.

# 14

## Finale at Buffalo Wash

'See if'n you can get on the roof,' called Santee. 'Looks like there's an opening up there. I'll keep you covered from down here.'

'Looks a mite tricky, Major.' Flannery was wavering. 'You sure we ain't bitten off too much with this caper?'

That was the last thing Santee wanted to hear.

'Ain't scared are yuh, Chip?'

''Course not,' answered the aggrieved young outlaw. 'But there's more'n enough loot stashed at the hideout for the both of us. Why not call it a day before things get too hot around here?'

Santee was silent as he mulled over the implications of Flannery's indecision. Maybe there was another way to skin a cat. He smiled to himself as a new plan began to form in his devious mind.

'Guess you're right at that, Chip,' he agreed, accompanying the remark with a heavy sigh. 'You get the horses ready while I keep these varmints busy. We can always set up a new gang when the dough runs out.'

'That's right,' replied a more upbeat Flannery. 'It sure makes a heap of sense.'

A few minutes later Lee heard the drum of hoofs coming from the direction of the outlaws' place of concealment. As he listened intently, it became clear that those remaining had had enough and were quitting the scene.

'They're getting away,' he shouted. 'The critters have given up and pulled out.' Without any hesitation, he went on, 'I'm going after them.'

'That very dangerous thing to do, my husband,' cautioned Chuan, holding on to him. 'Those bad men. Not hesitate kill good self if given chance.'

But the engineer was adamant.

'Don't worry,' he soothed quietly, resting a softened gaze on the anxious girl. 'I won't give them the opportunity to do me any harm.'

Duke Santee was not going to escape again. He had a big haul stashed away at the gang's hideout on Buffalo Wash, a haul that Lee Jago intended to commandeer for his own use. The bulk of it would still be there. Even a bunch of greedy galoots like the Rough Riders could not have spent it all in that short space of time. And didn't he deserve it after what he'd suffered at the hands of this bunch of skunks?

The only way of achieving that end was to follow the gang leader. Somewhere along the way he ought to be able to get the drop on him.

Lee had convinced himself that he was in the right. And nothing that Chuan Li could say would change his mind.

'You stay here,' he said. 'I shouldn't be gone more than a few hours. Buffalo

Wash is just over the other side of the mountains.'

'No can stay in this house of Hell,' she blurted out. An icy shiver trembled through her delicate frame as she cast a bleak eye around the bloodstained car.

Lee nodded his understanding.

'The gang must have set up a camp near by,' he said. 'Santee always arrived at a new hold-up site early to get the lie of the land.'

He carefully helped the woman out of the express car, then went in search of the camp. He was back in less than a minute.

'It's over yonder.' He pointed to a cluster of rocks, a loose smile playing around the craggy profile. 'The thoughtful jaspers have even left a pot of coffee on the boil.'

They both needed the boost afforded by the strong brew. Lee bound up the cut on his wife's head while trying to delay the final moment.

But all too soon it was time to leave.

Chuan hugged him close. A lingering

kiss was more than enough to convince Lee that this lovely girl deserved the best that life had to offer. And that meant a decent grubstake which was his for the taking at the gang's hideout.

With the greatest effort he tore himself away from Chuan's spellbinding embrace.

Spurring his mount across the undulating terrain of dry arroyos and gulches of the plateau, Lee soon caught sight of his quarry in the distance. They were unaware that a tracker was on their tail. And Lee made certain they remained in ignorance by maintaining a reasonable distance between them.

He had noted that there were only two riders. That would be Santee and Chip Flannery. Around noon a single pistol shot echoed down the draw he was following. It was too far off to have been meant for him.

What could it mean?

The answer was starkly revealed when he reached the crest of the next ridge. There, splayed out like a discarded rag doll, was the body of Chip Flannery. And, judging by the quantity of blood staining his once green shirt, he was obviously dead.

So that was Santee's game. The bastard wanted all the loot for himself. Flannery had always been a touch on the naïve side, too trusting by far. And it had been his undoing.

Barely according the unfortunate young gunslinger a second glance, Lee did not slacken pace. Indeed, he kneed the cayuse to a gentle trot. There was no time to lose.

Lee slowed his pace once he reached the banks of the Wash. Beyond the fringe of dwarf willows edging the far bank lay the concealed hideout. The loot had been hidden in a root cellar hollowed out beneath the floor of the cabin. Lee drew his pistol, tentatively nudging his cayuse through the loose covering of vegetation.

He paused at the far side. The cabin was fifty yards distant but the open ground offered no vestige of cover. Lee paused, unsure how to proceed. Anxiously he wondered whether he had arrived too late.

All around him the willows swayed and murmured in the low breeze. A collared lizard stuck its grey-and-yellow head out of a hole, sniffed the air, then disappeared. Time hung heavy as the minutes passed.

But it was another movement that caught Lee's attention.

The cabin door had opened. So confident was Santee that his nefarious scheme had succeeded that he failed to notice his pursuer edging across the open corral. Two heavy saddle-bags were slung across the outlaw's broad shoulders.

The Schofield gripped tightly in Lee's right hand was shaking. An engineer by profession, he was no gunfighter. But this varmint had to be stopped.

Lee swallowed hard.

'Hold it right there, Santee,' he hollered. 'Drop them bags and reach.'

Santee froze in his tracks. The face, wreathed in shadow beneath the broad hat-brim, visibly paled. Swollen peepers and a gaping mouth portrayed a startled expression. Momentarily the outlaw was nonplussed, confused. Pursuit across the arid badlands was something he had not reckoned on.

'I said drop them bags,' repeated Lee firmly. 'And no tricks. Nothing would give me more pleasure than to fill your mangy hide with lead.'

*The dynamite dude!*

How was it possible? Lee and that blamed wife of his oughta be dead. But this was no time for speculation.

Santee's brain had quickly thawed. Once again, he was thinking straight. Somehow this slippery jigger had escaped the fire and trailed him all the way from Zodiac Pass. Slowly the ageing hardcase turned to face his nemesis.

The guy was on the edge of the trees and well out of handgun range. Santee uttered a deriding laugh then continued his measured tread to where his horse was tethered. He had just swung the heavy bags across the leather skirt behind the saddle when a single shot rang out.

Santee hooted with laughter as a fountain of sand leapt from the ground where the bullet had struck. It was more than fifteen feet short. He drew his own pistol, spun the chambers and swirled the weapon on his middle finger in an arrogant gesture of disdain before slipping it back into the tied-down holster.

'You're gonna have to do a sight better than that, mister,' he bawled.

Lee suddenly realized that he was out of range. He lengthened his stride, then stopped to take aim. But just when he needed it most, the gun misfired. A bullet had jammed in the cylinder.

Ripples of dread coursed through his veins.

Santee took full advantage of the sudden change of fortune. Whipping out the .45, he snapped off a single shot. Lee cried out, grabbing for his leg. Assisted by a liberal dose of fear, the injured man hobbled back to his mount. But Santee had smelt blood. And he fully intended to bury this critter once and for all.

Another two shots split the ether. Both struck Lee's horse in the head. The animal let out a distraught whinney, then staggered, its forelegs buckling. Unable to scramble away in time, Lee was trapped beneath the animal's dead weight.

Santee uttered a deranged howl of triumph. His six-shooter bucked twice more, the bullets thudding into the horse behind which Lee was cowering.

'Prepare to meet your maker,' growled the outlaw as he closed the distance between them. 'This is the end of the line, mister.' A demented guffaw spluttered forth as Santee rejoiced in his superior skill. 'Now ain't that a good one.'

But Lee was not listening. Panic had gripped his very soul. Sweat poured down his face as stiffening fingers manically clawed at the buckle securing his saddle pack.

He had one chance. And that was all he would get.

Santee's grinning maw was getting closer. Lee could see the outlaw thumbing fresh rounds into his revolver.

Then he had it. The engineer mouthed a silent prayer, thankfully noting that the stick of dynamite was already primed. He delved into his vest pocket, pulled out a vesta and flicked the red tip with his thumb. It snapped off in his trembling hand.

'Noooo!' exclaimed the distraught engineer. 'Please. Not now!'

Santee had halved the distance between them. His pistol was raised to deliver the last rites.

A second vesta flared. The welcome burst of flame was instantly placed against the five-second strip of fuse wire. Lee blew on the glowing end. Suddenly it began hissing and crackling. He drew his arm back and flung the deadly stick at the approaching enemy.

Spinning like a crazy fircracker, the lethal charge seemed to float on the desert thermals. So self-assured was Duke Santee that he only perceived the fatal fiery rod in the final seconds of its descent.

His mouth dropped, black eyes rimmed with horrified fascination.

Too late, he turned and ran.

The dynamite struck his head, exploding on contact. A frightful scream of terror accompanied the monumental blast that ripped apart the stillness of Buffalo Wash. Lee hugged the ground behind the cadaver of his horse. The cataclysmic force generated by the explosion shook the ground. Sand and ragged bits of dripping flesh rained down on his cringing form.

For a full five minutes Lee kept his head buried in the still-warm back of his horse. Only when he was sure that he was still in the land of the living did he open his eyes. Jamming his good leg against the back of the horse, he gently levered himself out from beneath the dead animal.

Smoke and dust hung in the static air.

Of his adversary there was no sign. Lee drew his left hand across the warm, sticky wetness of his hair. It came away clutching a lump of soft matter. Peering down at the glutinous tissue, he suddenly realized what he was holding. His sallow complexion drained.

One of Duke Santee's bulging eyes stared back. All efforts towards self-control were abandoned as Lee's stomach lurched. Only when his heaving guts had finally settled did he feel capable of leaving the gruesome site. Bloody remnants merged with the ochre sand clinging to his boots.

But of the horse over which Santee had thrown the saddle-bags there was no sign. It must have been terrified by the explosion and bolted. A sudden jolt of pain was a stark reminder that he needed to stanch the loss of blood from his damaged leg.

Penetrating the dim interior of the empty cabin was a macabre and strangely unreal experience for the engineer. Recalling his last sojourn brought back unpleasant memories that he quickly shrugged aside.

He found a bottle of iodine and splashed a generous measure on to the wound. Then he bandaged it up tightly.

For the rest of that afternoon Lee scoured the countryside searching for the animal and its valuable load. As time passed it became an increasingly painful task. But he was determined to find the elusive hoard. Only when the shadows of approaching dusk threatened to curtail his pursuit did he eventually spot the animal. It was grazing on a clump of gramma grass next to a splay of cholla cactus and catclaw.

Not wishing to startle the nervous creature, Lee approached it slowly mouthing gentle words of encouragement. Eventually he was able to mount the horse. Darkness had embraced the harsh landscape by the time he returned to the cabin at Buffalo Wash, necessitating a forced overnight stay. Not a comforting notion, but there was little choice.

The hours of darkness passed in a series of brutally distinct nightmares which left the injured man bathed in pools of sweat. The arrival of dawn came as a relief.

After brewing a pot of strong coffee and chewing on a hard stick of jerked beef he set off on the long ride to Zodiac Pass.

Chuan Li had also spent a fitful night in the open. Huddled beneath a discarded and extremely rank saddle blanket, she greeted the dawn with relief, having slept nary a wink. Her drawn features registered the profound concern she felt on account of her husband's failure to return.

Later that day Chuan picked out a hazy mirage on the horizon. A single rider plodded wearily out of the searing heat of the desert. He dismounted and tumbled into her outstretched arms.

Total exhaustion had, at last, caught up with Lee Jago.

Chuan led him over to the campfire, sat him down and dribbled water on to the swollen lips. After all the excitement of the previous two days, he was exhausted. But the Chinese girl had spent her early years as a doctor's assistant. Immediately she set about cleaning and dressing the wound. Luckily the bullet had gone straight through the muscle. Quickly and expertly she stitched up the gash in his leg.

★  ★  ★

On the following morning Lee opened his eyes to behold a sight that he had feared never to see again. His wife's soulful expression was manna from heaven to the injured man.

His pale face cracked in a thin smile. 'I seem to be making a habit of this,'

231

he croaked. 'Thought I'd . . . never see you . . . again.' The halting words barely emerged above a hoarse whisper. 'But I got the dough.' A tremulous finger pointed to the saddle-bags slung across his horse. 'And Duke Santee sure won't be bothering us again.'

'Easy now, my husband,' she soothed. 'Eat broth. Get strength back quicker.' She gently spooned the warm mixture into his mouth.

'Tastes good,' he said. 'Be a sight better when we reach Canada.'

It was another day before they were at last ready to leave the gruesome battle site. Huojin Soo, and his loyal fireman, Crank Tanner were buried beside the railtrack. The bodies of the outlaws were left for the scavenging predators of the desert to dispose of.

'Gonna be a fine old mystery for the railroad bosses to figure out when they happen across this abandoned old loco,' remarked Lee from the bed of the flatbed wagon they had decided to use. His hand rested on the bulging leather bags beside him. 'Not somep'n for us to worry our heads over.'

'Good story for children though,' added Chuan Li, yipping the horses into motion.

'But with the bad bits left out,' added her sombre husband as they passed the two crosses, each sporting a blue-and-white striped cap.

Momentarily the buoyant mood dimmed.

A temporary pause for thought as the poignant realization dawned. Wasn't it an undeniable fact that Lee Jago and his wife had perished in that unfortunate accident back on Moccasin Flats?

The notion brought a cheerful smile to the engineer's face. Once again his hand strayed to the saddle-bags.

'Don't you think on it!' admonished Lee's sternfaced wife. 'All money, every last cent, will be returned to company.'

Lee sighed, then gave a resigned shrug. His gaze focused on to the northern horizon where the open trail promised new opportunities, a fresh start.